D1112642

The Boy from Over There

The Boy from Over There

Tamar Bergman

Translated from the Hebrew by
Hillel Halkin

Houghton Mifflin Company
Boston   1988

JF
B

Library of Congress Cataloging-in-Publication Data

Bergman, Tamar.
   The boy from over there.

   Translation of: ha-Yeled mi-shamah.
   Summary: Avramik, a young Holocaust survivor, has
difficulties adjusting to life on a kibbutz in the
days before the first Arab-Israeli War.
   [1. Holocaust survivors — Fiction.   2. Kibbutzim —
Fiction.   3. Israel — Fiction]   I. Title.
PZ7.B45223Bo   1988   [Fic]   87-36634
ISBN 0-395-43077-1

Printed in the United States of America

P 10 9 8 7 6 5 4 3 2 1

copy 2

THE MIDDLE EAST 1947

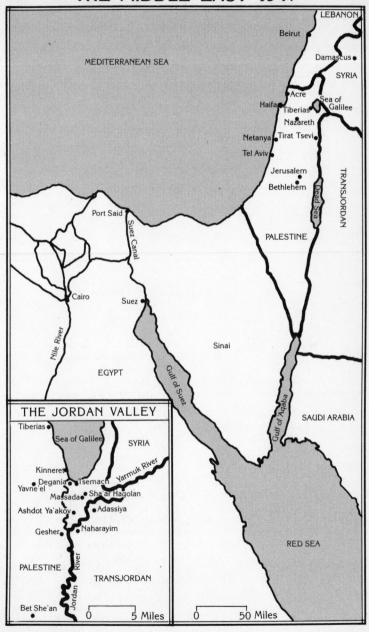

The Boy from Over There

1

"They're coming! Honest, they're coming!"

The kitchen workers rushed outside like a flock of pigeons from their roost and ran toward the front gate. From her perch on a high branch, Rina looked down on the kibbutz below. The center of it was empty. The kitchen staff had been the last to leave because they had prepared the welcome-home feast.

"Rina! Rinaleh!"

Rina's mother was coming toward the children's house. Dubik, Rina's three-year-old brother, was clutching Ma's hand and trying to drag her back the other way.

"Ma, that way. They all went that way. I want to go there too!"

How stubborn he could be. A regular little mule. Just yesterday he had been in diapers, and now he expected the whole world to stand at attention whenever he stamped his foot.

"One minute, Dubik. Just one minute," said Ma. "We'll go as soon as we find Rina."

They entered the children's house.

"Rina! Rinaleh! Where are you?"

Rina peered down through the glossy leaves of the

pipal tree. Her mother's voice echoed through the empty rooms. It was strange how lonely a voice could sound when no one was listening.

"Rina! Rinaleh!"

"Ma!" Dubik wailed. "Ma, that way! They're all there."

Rina's mother gave in. "All right, Dubik. Let's go. Maybe Rina is there, too."

She came back out of the children's house still holding Dubik by the hand and passed under the tree. Rina didn't move. She watched them hurry off. Soon they disappeared behind the large dining hall.

Thank God for that. What a pest. And her mother — Why did she always seem to be under such a black cloud? Why didn't she get rid of the line that had appeared on her forehead? Rina's father would come back. He had to! What would he say when he saw her mother so pale and unhappy?

It was the time of afternoon when the big lawn was usually noisy with grown-ups and children playing tag, hide-and-seek, and other games. Today, though, everything was different. It had started in the morning when their teacher, Alona, entered the classroom, flushed with excitement.

"They're coming. Our prisoners of war are coming home today!"

The whole second grade jumped to their feet and began to chatter all at once like the sparrows in the yard until Rami — freckled Rami with his shock of fiery hair — made them quiet down by saying proudly, "My dad's in the Jewish Brigade. He's not coming

2

home today because he wasn't taken prisoner. He's still got a job to do in Europe."

"What kind of a job?" asked little Naomi. "Why does he have to work there when he can work right here on the kibbutz?"

"What a birdbrain!" Rami jeered. "My dad's a soldier. He was in the war, but now that it's over his job is to help round up Jews and bring them to Palestine. But what do you know about it, you little shrimp —"

Rami and his big mouth! It took even less than that to make Naomi cry. "That's not so," she protested, her cheeks already wet. "I'm not a shrimp! I'm almost as big as you. I'm . . . I'm . . ."

Alona hugged her and stroked her curly hair. "There, there. Don't cry, Naomi. You are big. You're just a little shorter than the others. You'll see how you'll shoot up and be the biggest in the class some day. And you, Rami, have picked a fine time to open your mouth —"

"But she never understands anything," moaned Rami.

"I do too!" Naomi shot back from the safety of Alona's arms, her angry eyes glistening with tears. "Everyone knows that we were fighting Hitler. Some fathers went to fight for England —"

"In the British army." Alona corrected her.

"In the British army, and some stayed behind to watch over us. My father stayed behind and he's chief of civil defense. He's the most important person on the whole kibbutz because he's in charge of all the

3

guns. He has lots of them and your father only has one."

"My father fought the Nazis!"

Alona intervened. "Hold on. What kind of argument is this? Everyone did his duty: those who stayed behind and those who went to fight. And now that the war is over the soldiers of the Jewish Brigade have a new job: to help find all the Jews who survived the concentration camps."

"And those who hid, too, right?" said Ofra.

"Right," said Alona. "Some Jews managed to live through the war in hiding, and now they have to be found and brought to Palestine. That's what Rami's father is doing and why he won't be coming today. The two fathers who are coming home were prisoners of war who were freed."

"And mine too!" Rina called out. "My father is coming home too."

There was an awkward silence. Some of the children stared down at the rug while others looked to Alona for help. On the sill outside the window a pigeon sat plaintively cooing: "Gru-gruuu-gru-gruuu!"

Alona went to Rina and laid a hand on her shoulder. "No, Rina. You know that your father isn't coming today, don't you? You know that . . ."

Rina knew. She knew that her father would never come home again. That's what her mother had told her the day the line on her forehead had appeared, that her father would never come back from a faraway place called Italy. "Killed in action," it was called. But Rina didn't believe it. "They're wrong," she kept telling her-

4

self. "All of them. They don't know that my father's not dead at all. He was taken prisoner, too, and he's coming home with the other fathers. He's coming today!"

She slipped from Alona's arms and ran from the room. The children looked for her in every nook and cranny but couldn't find her. But then they had stopped, because the whole kibbutz had gone to welcome the returning prisoners. Even her mother and Dubik were there, waiting by the big front gate.

And Rina? Rina sat on a branch of the big pipal tree in front of the children's house. She didn't want to see the prisoners come home. Deep down she knew who would not be among them, though she still prayed for a miracle. And miracles existed even if none of the grown-ups would admit it. They had to!

The cows were mooing in the barn. Above the rows of olive trees, golden in the sunset, huge flocks of starlings wheeled in a noisy circle. The little village in the heart of the Jordan Valley was silent with anticipation. On either side of the Valley, like the two winged shells of an oyster, the mountains stood listening intently. And the kibbutz, a purpling pearl in their midst, held its breath.

Suddenly a car honked in the distance, then another. The silence was shattered by a burst of applause, followed by cries of joy and singing.

Rina stayed in the tree for a long time, hugging the large branch. She would have liked to be somewhere else, or better yet, nowhere. The wave of joy was now sweeping from the gate to the dining hall. The kitchen staff ran up to open the doors, and everyone poured in.

5

A circle of dancers sprang up, followed by a second and a third. Through the open windows of the dining hall Rina could see them whirling around.

She shut her eyes and covered her ears. If only she didn't have to see, if only she didn't have to hear, but, as from a seashell, the din of voices kept stubbornly resounding in her ears. What were they so happy about? How could anyone feel that way when her father hadn't come home? Just wait till he did! Just wait . . .

Suddenly something told her she was no longer alone. Opening her eyes, she glanced down. "Oh," she cried, seizing the branch with both hands. She had nearly fallen off.

A man was standing by the tree trunk, a man she knew from somewhere, though she couldn't remember where. He was holding a boy by the hand, a boy she had never seen before.

2

The strange but familiar man stared up through the thick leaves of the pipal tree. 'Who's up there?" he called, his voice strange but familiar, too.

Rina didn't answer. Her heart was pounding.

"Why don't you come down?" the man called again.

"What sort of a welcome-home is this? Or do you expect me to climb up to you?"

She had better do what he said. Quickly she slid to the bottom of the tree. There was no point in hiding any longer. For a moment she stood quietly by the trunk, hoping whoever it was couldn't hear the drums beating in her body. Then she looked up and studied him. Why, he looked like . . . like the man in the snapshots that Rami's father had sent home from the Jewish Brigade. Except that the man in the snapshots was different: tanner, taller, spiffier, and so much prouder. He was always smiling, and a row of shiny buttons blazed a trail of glory down his chest.

The man standing in front of her was also tall and tanned, but his eyes were tired and lusterless, as though they had seen too much. He was not in uniform and his shirt hung carelessly out of his khaki pants.

Suddenly she knew who he was. But she didn't say so. Why did *he* have to show up on this of all days?

The man looked at Rina, who was busily wiping the last traces of tears from her eyes. Then he grinned and said, "You're Rina, aren't you? I hardly would have recognized you. Everyone grew while I was away in the Brigade except me."

She still said nothing.

"Don't you know who I am?"

"Yes," she said at last. "You're Misha, Rami's father."

"Right you are," said Misha.

"But . . ." Rina stammered. "They said you were over there in . . . in Europe . . . that only the prisoners were coming home today."

7

"Well, either this must be Europe or they were wrong." Misha was joking, but his eyes were not joining in the laughter.

"And you recognized me?" Rina asked.

"Yes. You . . . look just like your father."

Why did they always have to say the same thing to her? Not that looking like her father didn't make her proud, but why did they always have to say it as though she was all that was left of him and that it was lucky that she was, because they didn't believe he'd come back. And now Misha, too. He had been there himself, in Italy, yet he agreed with them.

"Who's that?" asked Rina, trying to change the subject.

"Oho," said Misha, his face lighting up. "This is my nephew. Avremeleh, this is Rina. *Dos iz Rina,*" he added in Yiddish.

The boy didn't answer. He merely looked down at the ground, staring at the magical point at the base of the tree where roots turned into trunk. Pale, thin, and hardly any taller than Rina, he clung to Misha like ivy to a wall. His tightly pursed narrow lips made Rina think he hadn't spoken for ages and had secrets he would never tell anyone.

Misha cupped the boy's thin shoulder with a hand. "I found him over there, in Poland," he explained. "I was given special leave to go look for my family. It's a long story, Rina. I'll tell it to you some other time."

"And Rami. Have you seen him?"

"What a question. Of course I have!"

"And he let you go off by yourself? If I —" She

8

caught herself just in time. If her father had come home, she wouldn't have left him like that. And she wouldn't have let him go walking with some strange boy so soon after he arrived.

"Rami allowed me just a few minutes," said Misha. "I told him it was important. Avremeleh was frightened by all the racket. He's not used to so many people. It took him a while to get used to me, too, but now he never leaves my side."

"Where will he stay?"

"I think we'll put him in Rami's and your class. He's actually a year older than you, but he doesn't know a word of Hebrew. I came here to show him the children's house."

"But what's there to show?" Rina wondered. "It's just like any other children's house."

"Do you really think the whole world is one big kibbutz? Don't tell me that you've never been to town, Rina."

Really, how forgetful could she be? She had been to town and knew that children slept and ate with their parents there. Every morning they left home for school, and every afternoon they came home again. Once, while visiting some cousins, she and her mother had slept in the same room. She would have liked to live like that always, just the two of them. In fact, she would even have put up with Dubik, her little brother, if only she and her mother could be together. But as soon as she returned to the children's house, she forgot all about it. Her friends were all glad to see her again and old habits were reestablished.

"Come," she said, reaching out a hand to the new boy as if making up for her foolish remark. "I'll show you the children's house. We have a great class."

The boy jumped back and hid behind Misha, where he remained despite the soft, soothing words that Rami's father said to him in Yiddish.

"What's he afraid of?" Rina asked in amazement. "Did I do something wrong?"

"No," Misha assured her. "You didn't do anything, Rina. He's afraid of everyone."

"But why?"

"That's a long story. I'll skip to the end of it and give you the answer in one sentence: he lived through the war."

"But so did I." As usual, she spoke without thinking.

Misha looked at her. He knew. He had guessed why she'd climbed the tree instead of going with the rest of the kibbutz to welcome the prisoners home. Yet how could he know what she felt? In fact, how could anyone tell what anyone else felt? You could count hours, days, years. You could see how long a road was or weigh a loaf of bread, but how could you measure anyone's pain or suffering or hunger?

"I'll try to tell you in a few words," Misha said then, as if he had made up his mind. "It's a good thing he doesn't know any Hebrew yet."

Misha sat on the balcony of the porch. Avremeleh huddled next to him like a frightened animal.

"He was there during the whole war. His father was taken by the Germans right away. They must have killed him in one of the camps. But Avremeleh and his mother, my sister, got away and hid for years, until the end of the war, when some of our soldiers found them in a cellar."

"So where is she now?"

"I never found my sister," said Misha. "I believe she's dead. She was very sick when the soldiers took her to a hospital and the boy to the refugee camp where I found him."

"Does he know that . . . his mother is dead?" asked Rina, her mouth dry.

"Yes, he was told. But something tells me he doesn't believe it. He only knows that a Jewish soldier from Palestine brought her to the hospital in critical condition. He doesn't remember the soldier's name and I couldn't trace it."

They heard footsteps on the paved walk. Rami, bright-eyed and ruddy-cheeked, appeared.

"Dad, your fifteen minutes are up. That's what I promised you, and now you're mine again, aren't you?"

"Of course I'm yours," said Misha, swinging Rami into the air. "Yours, your mother's, Arnon's, and . . . Avremeleh's." He put Rami back on the ground.

Rami stared at the unwelcome newcomer. Avremeleh looked up and then back down, like a window that opens for a moment, then shuts again.

"Okay," said Rami grudgingly, "but first you're mine."

3

"What an occasion!" crowed Ovadia, Naomi's father, who, with Misha, would sleep with the children that night. "Both the teacher and the housemother have come to say good night in person. A real occasion!"

"We've come to say hello to the new boy," Alona explained.

Rika, the housemother, opened the linen closet. "We have to make Avremeleh's bed, don't we?"

She took out a sheet and pillowcase and placed a chair by the closet. "Ovadia, would you get down a blanket from the top shelf?"

"Gladly," said Ovadia, climbing on the chair. "I'm at your service, Rika."

As he took down the blanket and gave it to Rika, he noticed Avremeleh watching out of the corner of his dark eyes.

"You just wait and see, young fellow," said Ovadia, who was in a fine mood. "Everything will turn out all right. Why, I'd be happy to fall into Rika's and Alona's hands myself."

Avremeleh cringed and stared at the wooden bench he was sitting on.

"What's the matter?" asked Ovadia. "Did I say something wrong?"

"No. He just doesn't speak a word of Hebrew," Misha explained.

"Good Lord, I should have realized that," said Ovadia, tapping his head to show it was as empty as a dried pumpkin. "And I don't know a word of Yiddish. Well, never mind. Pretty soon you'll be telling Hebrew jokes, Avremeleh."

"I wish he would," said Misha, patting the boy on the head. "I wish he would tell some jokes. Right now he's forgotten how to laugh, even in Yiddish."

"But what do you propose to do with him?" Ovadia asked. "He follows you around like . . . like a turtle following its shell."

"I'll be available," said Misha.

"At night, too?"

"Especially at night." Misha frowned. "That's when he needs me the most."

"But where will you sleep?"

"We've moved another bed into Rami's room for Avremeleh, and I'll sleep on a mattress on the floor. Rami, aren't you through yet?" Misha called in the direction of the showers. "I'm standing and waiting with a towel and you're wasting water."

"Here I come," shouted Rami, shutting off the faucet. Soaking wet, he appeared on the high shower step. "On your mark, get set, go," he cried, running into the outspread towel. Misha caught him, wrapped him up, and rubbed him dry from head to toe.

"A-a-a-a-h!" Rami grunted to the rhythm of the towel

13

strokes. "Am I glad you're sleeping in my room. No one else's parents ever sleep with them. Will you sleep here always?"

"No," said Misha, drying Rami's wet hair. "Only until Avremeleh gets used to being here and isn't afraid anymore."

Rami tossed his head. "I hope he's always afraid. I hope . . ."

Alona and Rika exchanged glances. "Come, help me make the bed, Alona," Rika said.

The two of them went to the next room. Four beds stood there: Rami's, Rina's, Naomi's, and a fourth that had a straw mattress with a striped cover on it. Rika and Alona spread a sheet over the last one.

"This won't be so simple," said Alona from her side of the bed.

"No. Rami hasn't seen Misha for ages — for at least a year," answered Rika, tucking in the sheet. "He needs Misha now. Of all the times to bring —"

"I really don't know how wise it was," said Alona. "There are some excellent institutions for homeless children. They were taking in children from Europe even before the war, and now they'll take the survivors of the camps. It might not have been a bad idea to —"

Rika arched her eyebrows. "What's gotten into you, Alona? How could you send a child like that to an institution? You can see for yourself how he tags after Misha like a puppy."

"Yes, he does," Alona was forced to admit. "He certainly is lucky, though. There are children who come from Europe without family, with no one here at all."

"There are even some who have family that can't take them in. You know how much harder it is in town."

"I suppose," said Alona doubtfully, "that it is easier to take in a new child on a kibbutz. We don't have to do extra washes or cook extra food for him. But still, don't forget that the children here grew up together. They've used the same bathroom and slept in the same room ever since they can remember. They'll have trouble getting accustomed to someone new."

"Especially someone who's been through so much," Rika added. It was her turn to be skeptical.

"And who doesn't even speak Hebrew —"

"That's right," Misha declared from the doorway. Avremeleh was clutching his hand. "It won't be easy, but he has an uncle here. Besides which, I have faith in you both. Just don't make a big fuss over him. Treat him quietly, without fanfare, all right?"

"All right," said Alona, smiling at Avremeleh. Yet when she reached out to pat his head he dodged, leaving her hand hanging in midair.

"Here's your bed," she said to him. "Good night."

Like a beehive when darkness falls, the children's house quieted down. The children finished showering and brushing their teeth and went to their rooms to visit with their parents before lights-out. The large common room emptied, except for the heaps of clothing carelessly thrown on benches, wooden clogs, and an odd smell of shower stalls, toothpaste, and Lysol all mixed together.

In Room 1 the children and their parents were still talking. They discussed the returned prisoners, the

15

welcome given them, and the general meeting planned for the next day, at which they would relate their experiences.

Rochi was singing a lullaby in Room 2. Not only her son Ehud, but everyone in that room was listening to her clear voice. It brought a sweet lump to their throats and made them feel as though soft veils were dropping over the world.

In Room 3 it was time for lights-out. Rina lay in bed with her eyes shut while her mother tucked her in and sat down next to her.

"I've got the most wonderful mother," Rina thought. "She didn't ask me anything. I'll bet she knows. I'll bet she understands why I hid in the tree. But why did she go to the welcome-home? Just because Dubik made a fuss? Unless . . . unless she didn't believe them, either. Unless she also thought that it was a mistake, that Father was coming home. Maybe that's why she went."

Rina opened her eyes. Her mother had a soft, wan look. Rina was tired, too. It had been a long day. Too long.

From the doorway came the bell-like voice of Rami's mother, Mira. "Good night, children. I see you're managing."

"You bet!" Rami jumped up in bed. "The new bed fits perfectly. And Dad's sleeping next to me on a mattress tonight."

"Yes, I know." Mira smiled. "Rika told me. It took me forever to put Arnon to sleep. He's so confused and excited. That's why I'm late."

Two dimples flashed in Mira's cheeks. She had

honey-colored hair tied in a braid, and full arms. "Arms like Mother Earth's," Misha used to say, because they were always open to hug every child or baby as though it was her own.

"Good night, son," said Mira, kissing Rami on the forehead. "Sleep tight."

"Mom, you're not angry that we've taken Dad away from you, are you?"

Mira shrugged. "Angry? No. There wasn't any choice. But I hope your cousin soon gets used to being without your father. And I hope that he'll give him some free time tomorrow morning."

She purposely didn't mention Avremeleh by name, but the boy seemed to know he was being talked about. He lay curled up beneath his blanket, his dark eyes darting suspiciously from person to person. Mira went to him.

"Good night, Avremeleh," she said, reaching out to stroke his cheek. "Have a —"

All at once the boy jumped up, stood on the bed with his back to the wall, and shouted, *"Du bist nisht mein mama! Du bist nisht mein mama!"*

A shiver ran down Rina's spine.

"What is he saying?" she asked her mother. "What is he shouting about?"

"He's saying, 'You're not my mother,'" Ma whispered to her. "That's what he's saying. 'You're not my mother.'"

17

4

Rina had a bad dream. In it she was climbing up the endless scaffolding of a construction site, gripping the metal rods. Far below, as though at the bottom of a well, colorless cars crawled sluggishly like beetles beside heedless, uncaring pedestrians.

"Ma! Ma! Wait for me!"

The robots at the bottom of the well didn't bother looking up. Her mother, who was sitting on a rooftop across from her, watching Dubik build something out of blocks, didn't hear her, either.

"Ma, wait! I'm coming!"

Her mother rose, took Dubik by the hand, and was wafted away by the wind, blowing about in it like a piece of paper until she landed on the sidewalk. Then Dubik's blocks took off, too, turning into a cloud. With a stiff rattle the cloud came toward Rina, closing in on her slowly. How could she escape it? She began to run. She fled, down a dark stairway, flight after flight, until at last — there was her mother.

Though Rina's mother smiled at her, her mouth and eyes were empty windows, blank spaces through which Rina saw hissing red coals. Her whole face was nothing but a smiling mask covering coals and ashes. No! Rina had to put the fire out.

"Grandma, come quick. Ma's on fire!"

"Don't you worry," said her grandmother calmly, looping some yarn on her knitting needle. "Don't you worry, Rina. We'll get you a new mother."

"But I don't want a new mother," cried Rina. "I want my mother. Ma! Ma-a-a!"

Someone was gripping her shoulder, shaking her. Rina fell backward in bed.

"Ma." She sobbed. "Ma."

A warm hand was holding her own. A small hand, not her mother's. She opened her eyes. Though the room was dark, the bulb in the hallway cast a faint light on her bed. The new boy, Avremeleh, was crouching by her side, his dim face a mysterious shadow.

"Did I talk in my sleep?" she asked, the tatters of her dream still clinging to her on all sides.

Avremeleh put a finger to his mouth. "Shhh!" he whispered. "Shhh!" He pointed to the ceiling as though someone was listening there. Rina sat up in bed. Something scraped lightly against the roof tiles, then stopped.

"What's that?" she asked, relieved that her dream was receding. "Oh, it's only the wind. It makes the branches scrape against the roof. They always do." Avremeleh slipped away.

Rina listened to her heart beat. The sound seemed to come not from herself but from a galloping horse. That endless scaffolding, and those hot, glowing coals.

Had she really cried out in her sleep? Had anyone else heard her? But no one else had woken. Had Avremeleh been up all along?

Rami's and Naomi's peaceful breathing rose and fell rhythmically. From the mattress on the floor came another sound, one rarely heard in a children's house. Rami's father was snoring loudly, breathing in like a saw and out like a bellows: in, out, in, out. It was funny but reassuring. Strange, what a grown-up's snore could do. Only Avremeleh was quiet, hiding under his blanket like a mouse in its hole. From what? And how long had he been awake?

The wind had died down. The branches were still. Even the crickets had fallen silent. The horse in Rina's heart had galloped far away. She felt snug and safe.

And then, morning light was shining in and birds were trilling from the tree by the window. Rika entered the room.

"Good morning, children. Rise and shine, Misha. How was it, sleeping down there on that mattress?"

Misha turned over and lay for a moment without moving. He opened his eyes a crack and closed them again. He seemed to have been in such a deep sleep that he didn't know where he was.

"What? What did you say? Who is that? Rika?"

"Who did you think said good morning to you, Misha? The Queen of Sheba?"

"And why shouldn't she have?" Misha growled sleepily. He propped himself up on one elbow and looked around. His hair was rumpled and the stubble that had grown on his chin overnight stood out sharply in the morning light.

"Was I bushed!" he said. "I slept like a sack of potatoes."

"Potatoes don't sleep," Naomi informed him. She sat up, looking at him curiously, her short feet dangling over the side of the bed. She had never seen a father wake up before, not even her own. All groggy, his hair a mess, and his cheeks like two fields of thorns, Misha looked funny.

"Yes, they do," said Misha, winking at Rami. "Did you ever hear a potato talk at night? Never, right? Well, that proves they must be sleeping."

"They don't snore, though," put in Rina.

Misha laughed. "Just what are you getting at?"

"I heard you last night," Rina said.

"That's impossible," said Misha firmly. "I never snore. You must have been dreaming."

"Ask Avremeleh!"

She'd done it again, gone and blabbed without thinking. When would she learn to mind her tongue? Misha threw her a quick glance, his face growing serious. "What happened? Avremeleh was up?"

"Y-yes," Rina stammered. "I mean, for a while . . ."

Avremeleh lay curled up in bed, sound asleep. Who knew when he'd dozed off? Could he have waited for dawn to break? Had he fallen asleep only on hearing the first birds?

Misha patted him gently. His big, rough palm covered the boy's pale cheek. Avremeleh opened his eyes. There was blind panic in them, the terror of a trapped animal.

Misha smiled at him. *"Do bin ich, Avremeleh. Do bin ich."*

The boy shut his eyes again. His face relaxed.

"What are you all staring at?" asked Rika. "Make your beds and go wash up. Breakfast is on the table."

She left to go about her business. It was just another day. For Rami, though, it was still a holiday.

"Good morning, Dad!" he cried, leaping onto Misha's back.

"Good morning, son," Misha answered, sitting up. With a single quick motion he lifted Rami high into the air, flipped him upside down, and set him on the ground right side up again. "Did you sleep well?"

"You bet! Will you spend all day with us, Dad?"

"I have no idea, Rami. It depends on . . . your cousin. If he settles down a bit and lets me go, I'll join your mother. She deserves to be with me a little, too, doesn't she? And I with her?"

Rami didn't answer.

"Hey, Dad," he said suddenly, "why's he getting dressed like that?"

Everyone turned to look at Avremeleh, who was sitting up beneath his blanket, pulling on his pants. Feeling their stares, he froze, as if he'd been caught doing something wrong.

"He's not used to being with other children," Misha explained. "He's embarrassed. Never mind, though. In the end he'll be just like you. Just try not to stare at him."

Rami shrugged skeptically. He glanced at Rina for confirmation, but she pretended not to notice. She finished dressing and went to wash. Avremeleh hadn't looked at her once. Did he remember what had happened last night? Or could it have been just a dream, a dream within a dream? There was no way of knowing.

5

The next morning, a lively discussion was taking place in the children's house. Standing with his toothbrush in hand, Giyora was saying in low tones, "What kind of weirdo did Rami's father bring us?"

"Why are you whispering?" asked Keren loudly. "He can't understand a word you say."

"That's right, I'd forgotten. Did you see what he did last night?"

"No, what?"

"He wouldn't take a shower."

"That isn't so," said Ofra, joining in. "He was just waiting for the rest of us to go to bed. He showered then."

"So what?" asked Ehud. As one of the biggest boys in the class, he could afford to be generous and understanding — when he felt like it, of course. "Do you think everyone grows up on a kibbutz? City kids aren't

23

used to washing together. Everyone there showers alone. Sometimes they even lock the door."

"And he's not an ordinary city kid, either," said Ofra. "He's been through the war."

"So have we," said Keren. "I can even remember sitting with kerosene lamps in the air-raid shelter. It was a world war, World War Two, and we're part of the world, aren't we? We were in it too."

"Yes," said Ehud, "but you can't compare what happened here with what happened in . . . in . . ."

"In Europe." Ofra finished his sentence. The two of them were allies today.

"Right. In Europe. Rami's father was there and he says we have no idea how awful it was. He says that Avremeleh hid out with his mother all during the war. For years and years."

"And all that time he never saw other children? For years and years?"

"Of course not. That's why he's so embarrassed."

"You know what, though?" Giyora's voice was down to a whisper again. "I peeked into the shower while Rami's father was helping him wash. He's got a chain around his neck, just like a girl!"

"You're kidding!"

"I swear! A chain with a Star of David. He hides it under his shirt, but I saw it."

The front door of the children's house swung open. In burst the morning light, and with it, Alona.

"Good morning, children!"

"Good morning, Alona!"

"What is this, a kibbutz meeting?"

24

"We were just . . . talking."

"Now's the time for breakfast, my friends, not for talking. Hurry up and finish washing. Who's on duty today? No, not classroom duty, kitchen duty. Keren? Good. Then tell everyone to come eat. What, no one's hungry? But you haven't eaten all night!"

They all sat around the low, square tables. Even Rami's father occupied one of the little chairs, looking for a place for his long legs.

"Dad, why's Avremeleh eating like that? Is he really that hungry?"

Avremeleh stopped in the middle of a bite. He stared down at the table, gripping his slice of bread so tightly that his knuckles turned white.

"Why are you all staring at him?" Rika asked angrily. "He knows you're talking about him. It's not nice."

Rami persisted. "But Rika, look how he's eating. He just grabs and swallows without stopping to chew. Look how he's nearly finished all the bread."

"Good for him." said Rika. "If he's hungry, he should eat."

"Children," said Misha in a low voice, "it's not ordinary hunger. You don't know what it's like to be really hungry, to be hungry for years. And you're lucky that you don't. He was hungry all through the war — nearly all through his life, in fact. That's why he's eating so much."

"It's not his stomach that's hungry," said Rina all of a sudden. "It's something else."

Misha looked at Rina as though for the first time.

"Rina's right," he said, remembering their encounter of the day before, when her cheeks had been wet with tears. "It really is another kind of hunger."

"But Dad, who wants to look at it?"

"Then don't. Try not to pay any attention. He'll get used to eating like you in the end. I hope so, anyway."

There was an awkward silence at the tables. The children ate without talking, or at least tried to. Naomi weakened first. She pushed her mug away and said, "I don't feel like cocoa today."

Then Shai asked, "What kind of eggs did they send us from the kitchen?"

"What's the matter with them?" Rika wanted to know. "What's with you all today?"

"I asked for hard-boiled eggs, not soft. Look how soft this one is. Phooey!"

"That's no way to talk about food," Keren scolded.

"You're always talking just like the grown-ups," Shai said angrily. "You're nothing but a parrot. Next you'll start telling me about the starving children in India. I know those stories by heart. You're a parrot, that's all you are."

"You're a parrot yourself," Keren shot back. "You're . . . you're . . ." She couldn't find the right word. "Monkey see, monkey do, that's what you are."

"That will do, children," said Alona. "Whoever's finished eating, please go to the classroom. It's getting late."

Alona was a stickler for schedules and the start of the school day helped her put an end to the argument.

✻

26

There were six double desks in the classroom. The sixth had been added the night before. The children took their regular seats in pairs. Five double desks were full, the sixth empty.

"Come, Avremeleh," said Misha. "Sit here."

Avremeleh hesitated.

"*Kim und setz zich do,*" Misha said in Yiddish. "Sit here."

Avremeleh crouched at the empty desk.

"Who wants to sit next to Avremeleh?" Alona asked.

No one answered. Shai looked down at his desk, Keren and Giyora were doodling, and Rami was staring out the open window.

"Who volunteers to sit next to Avremeleh?" Alona asked again.

Her eyes went from child to child.

"This isn't the time for a lecture on how to treat newcomers. I'm asking for the last time, who —"

"I will," said Rina, getting up from her place. She crossed the room and sat in the empty chair. Avremeleh looked up at her for the first time that morning. Were his eyes trying to tell her they shared a secret? Rina thought she might even have seen a smile in them. But then he looked down again.

Misha brought a chair from the next room. Avremeleh looked up again. "*Du kenst gayn,*" he said to Misha in Yiddish.

Misha broke into a broad grin.

"What did he say?" Rina wanted to know.

"He told me I could go," said Misha. "He's ready to get along without me for a while."

6

It wasn't easy getting used to Avremeleh's silent presence. And it wasn't for want of effort, either. On the contrary. At first the children tried getting him to play with them. On his first day in class, during recess, Ehud went over to him and asked, "Would you like to play dodgeball with us?"

Avremeleh returned a frightened stare and shrank in his chair.

"Here, catch," called Ehud, throwing the ball straight at him.

Avremeleh held out his hands in self-defense, but he was too late to deflect the ball and it bounced off his nose. With a cry of pain he jumped up and ran to the door. Alona, who was standing there, caught him in her arms.

"Where are you running, Avremeleh? What's wrong?"

Avremeleh struggled like a little wild animal to break free.

"What's this? Blood? From your nose? Rika!" Alona called. "Rika, bring me a towel and some cold water."

As though caught in a net, Avremeleh kept squirm-

28

ing, his frightened eyes darting this way and that, looking for a way out. Suddenly he bared his teeth and sank them into Alona's arm.

"Ow!" screamed Alona, jumping back. Avremeleh wriggled free, sprang through the door, and made a break for it.

Ehud stood there bewildered, his eyes filling with tears. "It wasn't on purpose, Alona. Honest. I wanted him to play with us. I thought he'd catch the ball."

Alona looked at her arm, breathing heavily.

"I know you did," she said. "I know you didn't do it on purpose. Neither did he. He . . . he . . ."

Rika entered the room with a wet towel. "Here, Alona." She looked around. "What happened? Who's hurt?"

Alona took the towel and wrapped her arm in it. "Rika, someone has to get Misha, quick. Avremeleh's run away!"

"I'll get Misha," Ehud offered. "I'm the fastest in the class. You'll see, I'll bring him right away." And off he sprinted toward Misha's room, his guilty conscience giving him wings.

By the time Misha appeared in the children's house a full-fledged search was on.

"He's not in the toolshed!" called Naomi from the yard.

"Maybe he snuck back in through the back door," Giyora suggested.

"Maybe," agreed Shai. "We'd better look in all the rooms."

"And under the beds," said Keren.

"And in the closets," added Shai. "He's thin enough to fit into them."

Misha just stood there, an odd expression on his face. "Children, what are you doing? Stop! Stop looking for him this minute!"

"But he ran away," Shai said. "He ran away."

"And his nose is bleeding," Rina added.

Misha's face changed. "You mustn't hunt for him," he said slowly but firmly. "You mustn't. He's not an animal to be trapped."

"But his nose —"

"Don't worry about his nose. Just don't look for him. He'll come back by himself. He's not a wild animal."

"Oh yes he is," said Rami all of a sudden. "He bit Alona."

Misha threw his son a quick glance. Rami's lips trembled. Everyone felt that Rami should have kept his mouth shut. Misha turned to Alona and Rika, who were standing, ashen-faced, in the doorway. "Isn't recess over by now? Alona, why don't you take the children back to class. Is your arm all right?"

"It's fine," said Alona, removing the towel. "You're right, Misha. Children, back to class. Recess is over."

Rika was still agitated. "What about Avremeleh?" she asked. Even lesser things made her fret.

"I'll stay outside," said Misha, looking around the yard. "Sooner or later he'll see me and come back. After all, it's probably me he's looking for."

*

At noontime, when they had all sat down to eat, the front door opened. Misha's large silhouette filled the doorway. Avremeleh was hiding behind his uncle and clinging to his hand. Warned in advance, the children said nothing.

"Enjoy your meal, my chickadees," said Misha, grinning at their bewildered faces. "Is there anything left for a little woodpecker?"

They all stole a glance at Avremeleh. No one spoke.

"Come, join us," said Alona. "We'll make room."

Rami jumped up from his seat. "Dad, you'll sit next to me, won't you?"

"Why not?" asked Misha. "Isn't that what there are two sides of me for?"

They began moving around and squeezing together until everyone was seated again. Avremeleh was so busy wolfing his food that he didn't even look at Alona's arm.

Several days later, during rest hour, a discussion took place in Room 2.

"Do you think he's still mad at me?" asked Ehud, who hadn't gotten over the incident of the dodgeball.

"Of course not," said Ofra. "He must have realized you just wanted to play with him."

"Then why won't he play with us now? He's not so new anymore. He should be used to us by now."

"Alona says it will take a long time," Keren said, "because he comes from over there, and whoever comes from over there is a little . . . funny."

Ehud rolled over on his back and studied the patches of light and shadow on the ceiling.

"You know what?" he said at last, in a different voice. "He reminds me of the puppy I once had."

"You mean Brownie?"

"Yes. I swear he does."

"Rika'd be awfully angry if she heard you say he was like a dog," said Giyora. "And Alona says we mustn't talk like that, even though he bit her."

"Well, he reminds me of Brownie anyway," Ehud said. "Not the way he looks. The way he acts. He won't go anywhere by himself. Do you remember Brownie?"

"Of course," said Keren, putting down the book she had been trying to read. "He ran after you as if you were his mother. He'd whimper like a baby when you left him."

"See?" said Ehud triumphantly. "Avremeleh's exactly like Brownie. He won't let Rami's father go anywhere without him."

"I think he's getting used to us," said Keren. "Yesterday he was away from Misha all day. Misha only came for him after rest hour, when we all go to our parents anyway. Brownie was a pain in the neck for much longer."

"Who says?" challenged Ehud. "You're a pain in the neck yourself."

"This whole room is one big pain in the neck," declared Rika, appearing unexpectedly. They were so busy arguing that they hadn't heard her coming. "You're keeping the other children awake. I'm taking all of your books away and drawing the curtains. If

32

you can't read quietly like big children, you'll just have to sleep like little ones."

Ehud turned over on one side. For a long while he lay there, studying the plaster on the wall.

"Keren can say what she wants," he thought. "I still say he's just like Brownie."

And Ehud was right. Avremeleh adjusted just like a frightened puppy. At first he went nowhere unless asked to; then he began reconnoitering the children's house, peeking into every corner; and finally he gathered the nerve to go outside by himself and even to wander to the far ends of the kibbutz. The unseen cord tying him to Misha grew longer by the day. Only at night did it shrink again, so that Misha continued to sleep on the floor in the children's house.

Life began to settle down, like a lake in which a stone has made ripples that keep spreading until they disappear, leaving the water so smooth that no one can guess that a stone was ever thrown. Until one day, when the ripples appeared again. Strange things began to happen in the children's house.

7

Rika had begun to notice that the leftovers from supper were disappearing from the pantry. They simply weren't there.

"They're growing children," she said to Alona. "They have healthy appetites. They scrounge everything."

Every evening the children left tomatoes, slices of bread, and triangles of cheese on the table. And, though Rika put it all in the pantry, in the morning it was gone. Only the tomatoes remained on the shelves.

"It's curious," Rika remarked, "that our midnight snackers don't seem to like tomatoes."

"Not everyone does," said Alona, who was pre-occupied with something else. In fact, she forgot all about it until one Friday morning when she opened the pantry to take out the cookies the children had baked the day before for Naomi's birthday party. The heavy tin was where she'd left it, bulging with promise. Picking it up, however, she had a shock. It was lighter than a feather, as though nothing was in it at all.

"Rika!" she called. "Rika, did you put the cookies in another tin?"

"How could I have?" answered Rika from the hall-

34

way. "We don't have another big tin. It has to be there somewhere."

"It is there," said Alona, putting the tin on the table and opening it. "It just happens to be empty. There's nothing in it."

"That's impossible," Rika exclaimed. She was busy dumping dirty linen into a large sheet. "It was full to the top last night."

"Come see for yourself. Either I've gone blind or else . . . or else . . . I don't know what else."

Rika finished tying the sheet and left it in the hallway.

"It's no joke," she said, staring at the empty tin. "It is empty!"

Alona looked questioningly about. "But who could have taken the cookies?"

Her glance fell on Naomi, who had been hanging around the kitchen since breakfast. Now she just stood there, staring wide-eyed at the empty tin and pouting with indignation. She looked at Alona and her eyes filled with tears. A moment later she let out a heart-rending sob of disappointment, the cry of a child to whom a promise has not been kept.

Alona quickly put her arms around her. "Never mind, Naomi. Don't cry. You'll see, we'll find the cookies yet. We'll ask the class about them."

But asking the class did no good. Not one child admitted to having taken them.

"Are you trying to tell us, Alona," said Ehud, "that one of us would swipe the cookies he himself helped bake? Why, we made them for Naomi's party."

"Everyone knew we were going to eat them today anyway," added Keren.

"It can't be one of us," declared Shai. "It must be a bunch of kids from another class. No one could have eaten so many cookies in one night by himself."

Rina listened in silence. "But someone could have hidden them," she thought. "He could have hidden them so as to eat them later, one by one."

As usual, Avremeleh was sitting next to Rina. She didn't dare look at him. Did he understand what they were saying? Though she had tried helping him with his lessons, he never spoke to her. And yet, though he kept silent, the gleam of understanding in his eyes grew brighter from day to day.

Rina said nothing. Since the night of her bad dream she had wondered when Avremeleh slept. It was always a struggle for Rika to wake him in the morning. And why was it that he alone had heard Rina that night? He must have been up. It was the only answer.

Alona's voice floated above Rina's thoughts. "Well, maybe you're right. We'll have to ask the other classes."

"But what about my birthday?" Naomi wailed. "Won't there be anything special?"

"There she goes again," Rami jeered. "Eight years old and still a crybaby."

Naomi cried harder. Now she'd been insulted, too. Rika, who had been listening while wiping the tables in the dining room, came into the classroom and said, "Come, Naomi, let's go to the main kitchen. They must have baked some cakes there for the Sabbath and I'm sure they'll let us have a nice one. Let's go see."

And that was the end of it. Or rather, it was and it wasn't.

The next month Shai and Rina had birthdays, too. It was a kibbutz custom for parents to rise early on their children's birthdays and leave a present for them on the chair by their bed. Sometimes they left candy, too, or a vase of flowers. When the birthday child woke up and found the presents, it was the perfect start to a perfect day.

On his birthday, when Shai opened his eyes, he found a gift-wrapped package with a note that said, "Dear Shai, Have a Happy and a Sweet Birthday! From Your Father and Mother."

"I'll bet it's chocolate," said Brochi enviously. "A whole lot of it. You'll give us some, too, won't you?"

"Hold on. How do you know it's chocolate?"

"Well, it's something good to eat, anyway. It says, 'Have a Sweet Birthday,' doesn't it?"

"So what? That doesn't mean anything. My mother promised me a book."

"Come on, open it," Ofra urged. "You're keeping us in suspense."

Shai sat down with the package on the edge of his bed and slowly undid the ribbon. Then he tore the Scotch tape and removed the wrapper. The paper made a great rustle but Shai took his time. This was his great moment. All eyes were on him. Was it chocolate or a book? A book or candy? Reaching into the wrapping paper he pulled out . . . a book! It was large, with colored illustrations and a picture on the cover of a man by a swampy river holding out a flower to a huge

37

red crocodile whose toothy mouth was opened wide.

"Wow! It's *Lubungulu, King of Zulu*. What a book," said Ofra.

"It's just what I wanted," said Shai. "My parents knew. What did I tell you?"

"But why did they wish you a sweet birthday?" persisted Brochi. "On a book you write 'Happy Birthday,' but the card also said 'sweet.'"

Brochi was right. Later, they found out that Shai's mother had also left chocolate by his bed — and that it had vanished.

That evening Rika spoke to Misha. "You're here every night. Have you ever heard anyone sneak into the children's house?"

"What on earth for?"

"We know someone's been taking the leftovers from supper. At first we didn't mind. We thought the children were raiding the pantry. They're on a growth spurt now. But it seems that no one has been snacking after lights-out. They're too full of the candy they eat every day at their parents' to be hungry at night."

"Then who's been taking the leftovers?"

"I have no idea. That's why I'm asking you."

"To tell you the truth," said Misha, "I sleep like a log."

"You didn't hear Shai's mother bring him a present early this morning?"

Misha shrugged. "How could I have? Shai sleeps in Room One at the far end of the hallway. His mother wouldn't have come near my room."

"Meaning," said Rika despairingly, "that you don't know who took Shai's chocolate."

"Someone took Shai's chocolate? But Elka must have left it on her way to work this morning. That doesn't leave anyone much time to have made off with it."

"Precisely," said Rika. "That's why I think it was someone from the class. The problem is that no one will confess."

Misha's eyes searched for hers. "So you want me to stay up and catch the thief?"

Rika avoided his glance. "No," she said uncertainly. "Not yet. Let's wait a little longer. Next week is Rina's birthday. If it happens again, we'll have no choice but to —"

"Nab him! I wonder," said Misha, scratching his head perplexedly, "who it can be. I certainly am a heavy sleeper. Before I know it you'll convince me that I snore, too."

8

Rina lay in bed, staring into the darkness. The weak light from the hallway fell on pale shapes in white blankets that reminded her of cocoons. How odd to see three cocoons in white envelopes, each lying on its own shelf. Who had put them there? Why? When would the butterflies hatch?

From the floor came a sudden sigh, followed by a mutter and loud snore. Someone turned over on a mattress. Misha. Rina was wide awake in her corner of her room in the children's house. In the other three corners were Rami, Naomi, and Avremeleh.

The window was pitch black. It was still night. What, then, had woken her? She hadn't even been dreaming. And then she remembered: her birthday! Early in the morning her mother would come to leave a present, candy, maybe even flowers, by her bed. She must stay awake. She must be on guard. There was a candy thief on the loose, someone who —

Something snapped the thread of her thoughts. Through the open window came the call of a bird, a warble so thin, clear, sweet, and lonely that it sent a shiver through her. The first early bird of the day had awakened. From far off, like a little silver flute, came an answering call, solitary and searching. And as if the two together had brought the dawn, the dark patch of the window began to grow lighter, turning into navy blue velvet. Again the first bird sounded a long, yearning warble; the second bird answered and was joined by a third and a fourth. Soon whole choirs would come to life, accompanied by the farm sounds of the kibbutz: tractors going to work, a motor starting up, the blast of a horn, the sound of children. Now, though, when the window patch was still such a deep blue . . .

Slowly, cautiously, the door opened. Someone was

40

coming down the hallway. Rina's mother! Even when her mother tiptoed, Rina recognized her walk.

Rina shut her eyes and pretended to be asleep. She heard her mother approaching. She passed the first room, the second. Now she stood hesitantly by the door. She stepped carefully over Misha lying in the middle of the room and stopped by Rina's bed. Something rustled, something was put down, something was moved, and then, silence. Had her mother gone already? Rina opened her eyes a crack. No, she was still there, standing by Rina's bed and looking at her. Rina almost reached out to hug her. How she would have liked to be an only child again, without her brother Dubik, who wanted his mother all for himself. But she didn't move. Her mother wished to surprise her, and surprises must not be spoiled. Yet she wanted so much to reach out . . .

But her mother was no longer there. The sound of footsteps receded down the hallway, a door opened and shut, and she was gone. Rina could open her eyes now and peek, as long as she didn't move. The chair by her bed was spread with a white cloth, and on it was a vase of flowers, a mysterious present, and some candy. She mustn't touch them, though, mustn't move, so as not to give herself away. She must find out who the thief was, because otherwise . . .

Someone stirred in the bed opposite hers. Avremeleh. He slipped out from under his cover, sat up, and stood noiselessly on his feet. Warily, like a cat, he remained motionless for several seconds. Rina watched him through slit eyes. He began to glide across the room: a step, a second step, a third. Halfway across the room, he stopped again. Though the pale light falling through the window lit his face, his eyes were dark. They were glued to Rina's chair with its surprises.

How long did he stand like that? A minute? Two? Five? Suddenly he was awakened from his trance by a ripple of bird calls from the pipal tree outside. Slowly, as if dreaming, he turned and went back to his bed. Kneeling on the floor, he groped under the mattress for something. Then he rose, got back into bed, and pulled the blanket up over his head, a puppy safe in its litter. What had he taken from under his mattress? What had he done there? How could she find out?

A familiar sound of heels clicked on the pavement outside. The first kibbutz members were going to work. "Here we are," their heavy shoes tapped out. "Everything is all right. Don't worry, Rina, it's still early. You still have time to sleep . . . to sleep . . . to sleep . . ."

Then it was full daylight, the sun was shining in the window, and Rika was smiling by Rina's bed. "Happy birthday, Rina! I see that your mother was here before me."

Rina looked at the chair. It was all there: the flowers, the present, and, yes, the candy, too. She glanced at Avremeleh. He was fast asleep in his bed.

Halfway through the second lesson Rina rose from her seat, apparently to go to the bathroom. Rika was off somewhere, and the children were all bent over their books. Once in the hallway, she turned and headed for her bedroom. How quiet it was there without any children. A light breeze ruffled the curtains and sunlight spilled over the floor like thick, golden honey. The room had been cleaned and everything was in its place.

She went straight to Avremeleh's bed. For a moment she paused, glancing back at the open door and listening. Then she knelt quickly and lifted the straw mattress. It was just as she had imagined: squashed cupcakes, candy wrappers, and great quantities of bread — slices and slices of it, most of them stale, some covered with mold — all lying on the canvas between the bed springs and the mattress, icky and crumbling.

"Rina, what are you doing here?"

Rina froze. Rika was standing in the doorway! Rina dropped the mattress and stood up. Without a word Rika went to the bed, lifted the mattress, and leaned it against the wall. The secret cache stood revealed, like a burrow unearthed by a shovel.

For a long while no one spoke. Rina's mouth was dry from anxiety and excitement.

"Did you know about this?" Rika finally asked.

Rina shook her head.

"So that's why this room has been smelling so strange," said Rika. "I've been meaning to give it a good cleaning, to take all the mattresses outside and spray —"

"Yes, I know," blurted Rina. "You told me."

Rika studied her. "And you wanted to tell him? To warn him?"

Rina felt all confused. "I . . . I don't know," she

murmured. "I just . . . I wanted to know if it was really what I thought. But I didn't know what I'd do. If I'd warned him, he'd have known that —"

"That you had discovered his hiding place, right?" Rina nodded.

"He didn't take your candy," Rika said, half asking a question, half stating a fact. She looked at the buried treasure and mused aloud. "What do we really know about him? We've been told that he went hungry for years. And now he's afraid to be left without food, so he keeps hoarding it."

Rina shifted her weight from foot to foot impatiently. It was all too abstract for her. "But Rika, what do we do now? What happens when you take out the mattresses?"

"We'll have to throw it all out. We can't leave old food here. It's already gone bad."

"But Avremeleh has to hide it. You just said so yourself."

"I'm sure he'll move it somewhere else when he hears that we're doing a cleaning. He understands some Hebrew by now, doesn't he?"

"Yes, he does. But where else can he hide it? Do you want him to put it on his clothes shelf?"

"Good Lord! The idea!"

"Then maybe, maybe . . ." An idea was on the tip of Rina's tongue. "I've got it, Rika! Do you remember that big old bread box we used last year?"

"Yes . . ."

"Where is it? Did you throw it away?"

"Of course not. It's on the top shelf in the storeroom."

"Then maybe . . . maybe you could give it to him as a present, along with a lock and key. So that it could be his. His very own."

Rika thought it over. "All right, Rina," she said at last. "But on the condition that it's you who gives it to him. You'll know what to say to him."

Avremeleh did not know what to make of the big metal box. He ran his fingertips over it, carefully raised the rounded lid, lowered it, cast Rina a questioning glance, and looked back at the box again. Next to it lay a brand-new lock with a key in it.

"It's for you," said Rina, trying her best to sound casual. "I don't need it anymore. Do you want it?"

Avremeleh nodded quickly.

"Then take it. You can keep the key on your chain, next to the Star of David."

The boy's hand flew to the chain beneath his shirt.

"Would you like me to unhook it for you and slip on the key?"

Avremeleh gripped the chain with one hand and shook his head. All of a sudden he took the box, grabbed the lock and key, and ran off.

Rina felt an unexpected twinge of anger. "He could at least have said thank you. I'm sure he knows how to talk. He simply doesn't want to, that's all."

From that day on the box stayed under Avremeleh's bed, shut and locked. On the day of the big cleaning there was nothing beneath his mattress at all.

No one could recall exactly when the leftovers stopped disappearing from the pantry. The birthday candy, too, could again be safely left by the beds. What everyone did remember, however, was that on Rina's birthday, Misha stopped sleeping in the children's house. Avremeleh, it seemed, no longer needed him at night. The cord between them was long and strong enough.

Rami, too, remembered that his father stopped sleeping in his room on Rina's birthday, but he saw no reason to be happy.

9

Rami began to spend long hours in the stable. Sitting on a fresh stack of hay, his arms around his knees, he kept his eyes on Star's new colt. Though just a few days old, he was already quite lovely with his long, wobbly legs, his brown velvety coat, and his large, curious, almond-shaped eyes.

Only Rami and Brochi knew about him. Eliahu, Brochi's father, was in charge of the stable, and it was he who had secretly told Brochi that Star had foaled. It had to be kept a secret because, if everyone found out and came running at once to see the colt, it would frighten Star. So Brochi had told only Rami, no one else, and since then Rami had spent all his free time in the stable.

When Eliahu let him, Rami brought Star fresh bran and changed her drinking water. He liked being in the stable with Star and her colt; he liked it better than being in his parents' room, where Avremeleh hung around all afternoon, clinging to Rami's father like a little monkey and never leaving him for a minute.

There were four people in Rami's family: his father, his mother, himself, and Arnon, who was born a short while before Misha volunteered to fight the Germans, in the Jewish Brigade. Arnon had annoyed Rami endlessly by demanding most of his mother's time while Misha was away, but now that Misha was home again, Rami didn't care that the little crybaby was always with his mother. He, Rami, wanted his father — and he wanted him all for himself. The problem was that his father had brought Avremeleh home with him, and Avremeleh tagged after him everywhere.

You weren't allowed to fight with Avremeleh, either. You weren't even allowed to be mad at him.

"What do you know about it?" Rami would be told. "What do you know about what he went through?" or "But you were never hungry, really hungry, as he was." or "The child is an orphan. He'll never have a father or a mother of his own."

What could you say to grown-ups who told you such things and always gave in to him? They let Avremeleh get away with everything.

The colt tottered, trying to stand. Star arched her neck and licked his back with her warm tongue. Quick ripples of pleasure ran through his velvety coat. He lowered his head and began to nurse greedily. What a darling.

Who could blame Rami for liking the stable? In it he was far away from the boy who had stolen his father, far away from his class, and — yes! — far away from that pest of a Rina. What a little saint she was, sitting next to Avremeleh and helping him with his homework because it made her feel as if she was saving the world. "I swear," thought Rami, "it's all her fault that my dad stopped sleeping in the children's house." It was only because of her that Avremeleh didn't need Rami's father to be there all day and sleep on the mattress at night. So what if Avremeleh had followed him around like a leech? At his parents' this annoyed Rami, but in the children's house it was different. There it meant that his father was around all the time.

Rina was a spoiled brat. She, too, got away with everything just because she had no father, just because he had been killed in the war. The other kids in the class all stuck up for her. And they all picked on him, Rami.

Rami put his thoughts aside. Eliahu had entered the stable.

"I see you can't bring yourself to leave the colt, eh?"

Rami didn't answer at once. He swallowed hard, hesitated for a moment, and then asked, "Eliahu, may I pet the colt today?"

Eliahu thought it over. "No," he said at last. "I think we'd best wait until tomorrow. Star is very jumpy after foaling. If you make her nervous, she won't have enough milk for the colt."

48

"But is it all right to tell about it now?" asked Rami, getting up.

"I suppose so," answered Eliahu, filling a bucket with fresh water. "In fact, why not? The colt's already several days old."

"Yippee!" said Rami, trying not to shout too loudly. "I'll tell the whole class. I'll bet they'll all want to come tomorrow. You'll see, they'll all be here!"

Rami was right, of course. The next morning his class set out for the stable. There was a strong smell of spring in the air. The warm, bright sun that had brought forth masses of bright flowers in the gardens reflected off the red hair of the mechanic who was preparing the combine for the spring harvest and baked the dried black mud of the path into a webwork of cracks.

Eliahu was waiting for them by the entrance to the stable. "Shhh," he whispered, putting a finger to his mouth. "Quiet! Star is very nervous after foaling."

"If you scare her," said Rami, showing off his knowledge, "she won't have enough milk for the colt." That morning he was the happiest boy in the kibbutz. It was he who had told them all about Star's colt, even before Brochi, Eliahu's son.

The silent but excited children jostled through the entrance of the stable with Alona bringing up the rear. Enveloped in warm darkness, they slowly began to make out shadows and faint light from outside. The stable smelled of hay, manure, and fresh greenery. A whinny came from one corner. They all turned to look. There, on a clean, bright bedding of hay, lay Star, look-

49

ing at the children. Her big eyes were brown, moist, and shining with pride and vigilance.

"Wow!" Naomi whispered. "What a beauty of a colt."

"You said it," Shai agreed. "It's like out of a fairy tale."

Ofra pointed to a white mark on the colt's forehead. "Look," she said, "it's just like his mother's. Eliahu, don't you think we should call him Starry?"

"Maybe," replied Eliahu, not really listening. He was looking in amazement at Avremeleh, who was so excited that he kept gulping. His eyes were glued to the little colt and his hand reached out to him longingly.

"Would you like to pet him?" Eliahu asked softly.

Avremeleh nodded, his eyes still on the colt.

"Then go ahead," said Eliahu. "It's all right. Just do it gently."

Avremeleh stretched out a shy hand and lightly touched the brown velvety fuzz as if it were something magical that might disappear any moment. The colt quivered. Star looked up for a second, then went on licking the colt's back. Avremeleh drew back his hand and stared at the colt in wonder. His eyes were bright and the smile on his face kept getting bigger and bigger.

"Good," said Eliahu. "She's not afraid of you."

"May I pet him, too?" whispered Rina, who was standing next to Avremeleh.

"And me, too?"

"And me, too? May I pet him, too?" asked all the children in hushed voices.

Eliahu thought for a minute. "All right," he said. "But gently, one by one."

"That's no problem," said Alona. "They're already standing in line. Just don't push, children."

"I'm first," Rami announced.

"No you're not," said Alona. "It's Rina's turn, because she's next to Avremeleh."

"But," Rami protested, "I'm the one who told you about him. You're all here because of me."

"So we are," Alona agreed. "But there's already a line. Be patient, Rami," she added softly. "There are only four children ahead of you."

"But I was first inside the stable and I should be first now, too," Rami insisted loudly.

Star looked up nervously and got to her feet. Butting the colt to the wall with her head, she stood protectively over him, her ears pulled back tensely.

"Out," hissed Eliahu in a voice that no one could argue with. "Outside, all of you!"

The children gave a start and jostled back out through the entrance into the glare of the sun and the hot, noisy farmyard.

"It's all your fault," said Shai, falling on Rami. "It's your fault we didn't pet the colt."

"What do you mean, my fault?" Rami shot back. "It's Rina's fault. It's all because of her!"

"No it isn't. It was her turn."

"No it wasn't. It was mine."

"It was not!"

"I told you about it. I brought you to the stable. It was my turn!"

"It was hers!"

"She gets everything, the little brat! And it's only because she has no father, isn't it?"

The children sucked in their breaths. Rina turned pale and hung her head. She could feel them all looking at her. Rami had gone too far to stop. Raising his voice even louder, he shouted at Rina, spitting out the words one by one. "I'm glad your father's dead!"

For a second they all froze, as though under a spell of silence. And then something unexpected happened. Avremeleh leaped on Rami's back and began to pummel him, shouting, "Don' you say that! Don' you ever say that, you hear? I kill you! I . . . I . . ."

Rami toppled to the ground with Avremeleh still on top of him.

"Don' you ever say that!" he kept shouting, punching Rami again and again as though possessed. It was all Alona and Eliahu could do to pry the two cousins apart.

"That's enough, Avremeleh! That's enough!" cried Alona, shaking all over.

"I'm not Avremeleh!" screamed the boy, struggling to break free of Eliahu's strong arms. "And I'm not your friend. I'm Avram. Plain Avram. Avram!"

"Gee," whispered Shai to Ehud, "I didn't know he was so strong."

"That's not all we didn't know," Ehud whispered back. "We didn't know he could speak Hebrew, either. Who would ever have guessed?"

52

10

Two years had passed since the day of that surprise outburst, and no one mentioned it any longer. The children finished the school year, and then another. Having chosen the more Hebrew-sounding name of Avram, Avremeleh was now nicknamed Avramik. Everyone remembered, of course, the day he'd arrived, the day he'd let Misha leave him for the first time, and yes, the day he'd thrown himself on Rami and revealed that he spoke Hebrew. But since nothing very special had happened after that and time flowed quietly along, no one noticed the exact moment at which the pale, frightened little boy whom Misha had found in Europe at the end of World War II had turned into dark, quiet Avramik, who still kept aloof from his noisy classmates but was the fastest runner in the class.

Since that day in the stable Rami had left his cousin alone. A sort of truce prevailed between them, an unspoken agreement that was confirmed by time. To the onlooker, their relationship was like the smooth surface of an untroubled pond. Yet who knew what currents flowed beneath the surface? Who could predict what might happen? A sudden storm might be all that was needed to set them at each other's throats again.

The days and nights went by, days of hectic activity and nights of rest that never seemed long enough. One night alone, the night of November 29, 1947, was longer than usual. It was the night that the United Nations voted to divide Palestine into separate Arab and Jewish halves, that is, to create a Jewish state.

Only infants and toddlers slept at all that night. The fourth-graders stayed awake to listen to the vote. When the big radio, whose hoarse voice had been booming in the dining hall, announced the final count at last, the brooding tension suddenly lifted and the members of the kibbutz broke out in excited applause, in cries of joy, and in circle after circle of exhilarated dancing.

The next morning Rika woke the children later than usual.

"Good morning, you all. It's time for brunch."

"Brunch?" asked Giyora, peering out from beneath his heavy winter blanket. But Rika, as busy as a bee on a summer's day, was already in the next room, waking the children there.

"What happened to breakfast?" wondered Giyora, who never missed a meal and who — ever since Avramik had moved to another room — made up a foursome with Rami, Rina, and Naomi.

"It's late because it's Saturday and there's no school today," someone guessed.

"What kind of Saturday?" mumbled Rami sleepily. "It's not Saturday at all. It's Sunday. It's late because . . . because —"

"Because we went to sleep late," said Rina. "Because last night the United Nations voted us a state!" She would have preferred to curl up beneath the warm blanket again, but her empty stomach had other things in mind. "What difference does it make if you call it breakfast, brunch, or brupper — I'm starving. If you don't get up I'll eat it all myself."

"Not if you share it with me," said Giyora, getting out of bed too. "We'll eat it together."

Thus warned, the two other children in the room also rose quickly, and in no time the class was sitting down to eat.

Alona poured the cocoa, her face glowing.

"Alona, aren't you glad we'll have a state?" asked Shai.

"How can you even ask me that? Who isn't glad?"

"Well, then," said Shai, "shouldn't we make this a special day for everyone, especially for us children?"

"Isn't getting a Jewish state special enough for you?"

"Sure it is. And we even got up late today, like on a Saturday. So why not keep it up and make the whole day a school holiday?"

Shai was seconded by a chorus of shouts.

"Good idea!"

"Shai's right!"

"Who can study on a day like this?"

"Who wants to?"

"Quiet! Quiet, children," said Alona, looking at them with a mysterious smile. "Who said anything about school today?"

"Hurray!" cried Naomi, who was the first to get the hint. "Can we go to our parents, then?"

"No," Alona said. "The grown-ups are working as

usual today. Instead of studying, though, we'll go for
a —"

"Hike!" they all shouted together. "A hike!"

Alona's eyes shone. "You guessed it. We'll go to the
fish ponds by the Yarmuk River. I've already arranged
it with Misha, who's in charge of the ponds."

Rami was ecstatic. "Great! We'll show you the ponds.
I know them all because I go there with my dad every
Saturday."

Avramik, who had been eating and seeming to pay
no attention to the general gaiety, raised his mug and
asked, "Rika, is there any more cocoa?"

"Yes, there's still a bit left."

"Here," said Alona, pouring the last of the cocoa into
Avramik's mug. "But hurry up, we're leaving soon."

Avramik drained the mug and took another slice of
bread for the hike. Giyora, a chubby boy, looked at him
enviously. "You're a bottomless barrel," he said. "You
eat and eat and you're still as thin as a rod."

"And you're the bottom of the barrel," Rina answered
him.

"You and your jokes," Giyora said angrily. "They
never make any sense."

"They do too!" Rina retorted. "Alona, isn't there an
expression, 'to scrape the bottom of the barrel'?"

"Yes. It means to take all that's left of something."

"You see?" cried Rina. "That's you. You always take
all that's left."

The children in the little dining room burst into
laughter. But a minute later, when they all rushed outside for the hike, the joke was forgotten. By everyone,

that is, except Giyora, who never forgot anything, least of all an insult.

11

It was a bright, crisp day. The dark road, on which the mud had dried between the rains, ran straight as an arrow through the green fields. It headed steadily eastward toward the mountains of Transjordan, which had traded their drab summer frock for the bright green robes of early winter. Beyond the fields, across a babbling irrigation canal, the road suddenly dipped and zigzagged down a steep slope. The children stopped there, at the edge of the plateau, and gazed down into the Valley.

Far below, amid banks overgrown with reeds and lush plants, the Yarmuk River flowed gray and strong. Sprinting from its source, the narrow ravine that formed the border between Syria and Transjordan, it sped down into the Jordan River, carrying silt, broken branches, and other debris that the winter rains had washed into it. Beyond it, to the east, lay Arab villages of plain adobe huts without a bit of greenery, smelling of sheep and smoke from their outdoor cooking stoves. Along the west bank of the Yarmuk, at the bottom of the steep descent, the kibbutz fish ponds were arranged in neat rectangles like building blocks. Long dirt embankments ran among them, separating one from the other.

Avramik narrowed his eyes, squinting down at the ponds. "Look," he said, pointing at one of the embankments, "there's Misha."

Rami pushed forward. "Where? Where's my dad?"

"There," said Avramik, pointing again. "On the embankment behind the third pond. Near the 'Jungle.'"

The Jungle was the name given to the thicket of reeds and water plants that ran along the banks of the Yarmuk.

"Hey, it's him, all right," Rami announced happily. "I can tell by his clothes."

Rina marveled. "How can you tell by his clothes? The whole kibbutz wears the same work clothes!"

"Then by his walk," said Rami. "Honest, I know my dad's walk. And anyway, he said he'd be waiting for us down there, didn't he?"

"Yes, he did," Alona confirmed. "We agreed on it this morning."

"You see, it's him," said Rami. "Alona, I'm running on down to him."

Without waiting for an answer, Rami broke away from the group and began racing down the road. Several of the other children set out after him, all running together like a suddenly released spring.

"Watch your step," cried Alona after them. "And no shortcuts!"

But they were already beyond earshot and bounding down the hill like a flock of goats. The first to leave the road and cut straight down was Avramik. After him hurried Rami, Shai, and Ehud, with Keren not far behind. While the other children stuck to the zig-zagging road, the small band of five made straight as the crow flies for the fish ponds.

Avramik was the first to reach the embankment, where he stopped to catch his breath. Glancing toward the other end of it, he saw that Misha wasn't there.

"He's gone," he said to Rami, who came running up. "He must be at another pond."

"No, he isn't." Rami panted, speeding by without stopping. "I saw him head for the Jungle."

Avramik gritted his teeth and shot forward. Misha might be Rami's father, but that didn't make Rami faster than he was. No way! In a fair race no one could beat him.

Avramik quickly gained on his cousin. Rami's checked shirt danced before his eyes as he caught up. There! He passed him and kept running toward the Jungle. He was already too far in front to see Rami reach out a hand to push him off the embankment. The hand pawed the air and a second later Rami fell sprawling on the hard dirt.

"Ouch," he cried, rolling over with his knees drawn up. "Darn you!"

Avramik stopped, looked back, and retraced his steps. He knelt by Rami's side. "What's the matter?" he asked worriedly. "Where does it hurt?"

"In the knee, you jerk! Couldn't you have watched where you were going?"

Avramik, who hadn't seen what had happened

behind his back, didn't know what Rami was talking about. "But what did I do? I never touched you."

"You never touched me? You pushed me, that's what you did!"

"Say" — Avramik appealed to Ehud, who came running up — "did I touch him? Did you see me push him?"

Ehud pulled up short. He gasped. "Rami, come off it! We saw everything."

Rami glared at Ehud, turned his back on him, and rolled up his pants leg to look at his wounded knee.

"It's nothing," said Keren, arriving with Shai. "It's just a scrape. You'll feel better in a minute."

"No one asked you to play doctor," Rami snapped. "I know your type."

Before Keren could answer, a familiar figure emerged from the thicket by the Yarmuk.

Rami jumped up. "Dad," he called. "Hey, Dad, come here!"

Instead of approaching, Misha signaled with his hands.

"What does he want?" Rami asked.

"He's telling us to be quiet," Keren answered. "Something's happened down by the Yarmuk."

The children crouched by Misha's side in the lush growth by the riverbank; Misha's tense look kept them from moving. Naomi stayed close to Alona. She would have liked to hide like a baby kangaroo in Alona's pockets, had they been big enough.

"What are you looking at, Dad?" Rami asked in a whisper.

Misha pointed silently to the nearest Arab village across the Yarmuk.

"What do you see there?" Rami wanted to know. "It's just an Arab village."

"Be quiet and look," said Misha softly. "Try to see if there's anything different."

The children peered across the river through the tangle of reeds. It was high noon. The bright winter sun shimmered on the crowded adobe houses. The voices of women and children carried on the wind together with the pungent smells of sheep, smoke, and other scents that did not exist on the kibbutz.

Rina was the first to break the silence. "But it looks just the way it always does. There's nothing special."

"Are you sure?" asked Misha. "Listen."

They strained to hear. Misha was right. Mingled with the usual sounds of the village was another, more distant noise. It was coming closer, getting louder, until they could clearly make out the roar of a truck. Or maybe two. Or maybe . . .

Misha was staring hard at the dirt road winding down from the mountains on the horizon. The children followed his gaze up a soft hill, beyond which lay a hidden fold of ground. Everything seemed so familiar and yet so strange. It was the same valley as always. Across from them, on the other bank of the river, grew the same lush plants, the same rushes and sticky elecampane. The soil was the same soil, rich and heavy, the thick alluvial soil of the Jordan Valley. The road was the same muddy road, dried by the winter sun, no different from the road behind them that ran through the kibbutz alfalfa fields. And yet everything *was* different, unfamiliar, hostile, not their own. Everything was Arab.

The noise of the invisible motor grew louder, and suddenly, from behind the soft ridge line, a truck appeared as though out of the earth. For a moment it seemed to teeter on the hilltop; then, like a giant beetle, it started down the slope with its load. Behind it came a second truck, and then a third and a fourth, all heading down after it.

The village shook off its noontime slumber. Its inhabitants came running out of their huts with shouts of joy, gathering in the main square and pointing at the approaching convoy.

Alona's eyes turned from the village to Misha. His face wore an expression she had never seen before. "Misha," she said, "those trucks are the Arab Legion's! We'd better head back!"

"All right, Alona," he answered without taking his eyes off the village. "Take the children and start back. There's no knowing what will come next."

"Dad," asked Rami, "are you staying here?"

"Yes. I have to see what happens. I don't like the looks of this."

"Then I'm staying, too," Rami announced, sitting next to his father.

"No you're not!" said Alona. "You're coming with us and —"

Something whistled above her head and vanished into the bushes, something that someone had thrown. A second later something else flew in a low arch across the Yarmuk, landing at Naomi's feet. This time they saw what it was: a stone!

12

They swung around. In the low bushes across the river stood three Arab boys. They were children themselves, no more than ten or eleven years old, barefoot and unkempt, staring across the water at the group from the kibbutz. Ambling beside them, a flock of sheep and black goats was peacefully cropping the undergrowth along the bank.

"How did they get there without our noticing?" Naomi wondered.

"We were too busy looking at the village to see what was happening under our noses," Alona answered. And she added, firmly, "Children, we're going back. Right now!"

Before anyone could move from his place, though, one of the shepherd boys bent down, picked up another stone, and threw it hard and with sure aim. The children scattered. It hit the ground where they had stood a second before and rolled into the brush.

Misha stepped down to the riverbank and called out something in Arabic. The three boys smiled sheepishly but didn't reply.

"*Ya walad, mineyn jai?*" Misha called again.

The shepherd boys shrugged and glanced at one another as if deciding whether to answer. The biggest of them squatted on his haunches, his elbows propped on his knees and his chin cradled in his palms. His two companions did the same, so that together they looked like three firmly rooted plants.

"I think I know the big one," Misha said under his breath. "His father was a troublemaker too."

Rami, who couldn't stand even the mildest provocation, picked up a clod of earth and flung it back across the river. It sailed high in the air, fell apart over the water, and rained down harmlessly into the gray current.

The boys on the other bank burst out laughing and shouted some guttural words.

"What are they saying, Dad?" asked Rami, flushed with anger and shame. "What are they shouting at us?"

Misha hesitated. "They're just calling us names. Come on, let's get out of here. We have better things to do than have rock fights with Arab shepherds."

"But really, Dad, what are they saying? Why don't you tell them to clear out? Why don't you . . ."

Misha didn't answer. The boys across the river stood up again, their shouts now accompanied by coarse gestures. One of them turned and pointed back toward the Arab village. The children turned, too, following his arm. Yes. They had almost forgotten why they were there. The village had changed dramatically. Its central square hummed like a beehive and its black-cloaked figures had been joined by dozens of men dressed in khaki. Still others were descending from the trucks. Clearly, they were soldiers. The Arab Legion!

Seeing the kibbutz children stare at the village made the shepherd boys laugh and shout even louder. The wind bore their voices across the Yarmuk.

"Dad," Rami demanded, "why don't you tell us what they're saying?"

"They're saying that they'll drive us out of here," Misha answered at last. "That they'll take our kibbutz and chase all the Jews out of Palestine. That their soldiers will conquer everything."

As usual it was Naomi who asked the question that was on everyone's mind. "But why? Just yesterday the United Nations voted to divide the country between us. Alona explained that the Jewish parts of it will belong to a Jewish state and the Arab parts to an Arab state. So why —"

One of the boys on the other side of the river bent down, picked up a large rock, and heaved it into the current with both hands. Falling short of the children, it sent a cold shower of water over Ehud.

"Hey!" Ehud cried in surprise, as if only now realizing that he was not just an innocent bystander. "What do they think, that they're the only ones who can play rough? Come on, let's show them that we can, too!"

Before Misha and Alona could do anything, several of the children had picked up stones and clods of earth and begun throwing them at the shepherd boys. Pocking the dirty waters of the Yarmuk, none reached the other side.

Across the river the three boys laughed loudly, mockingly, again.

"T'fadel!" called the biggest, crossing his arms on his chest. *"T'fadel!"* Another stepped up to the water and spat. Misha tried to exercise restraint.

"Boys and girls," he called, "this isn't a game. We're all going back."

But it was too late; the children were out of control. They were all throwing stones across the river, calling out names as they did.

"Stop it!" cried Alona. "Stop it this minute!"

"We'll show them," shouted Rami and Ehud. "We'll show them what —"

A well-aimed stone from across the Yarmuk hit Keren in the leg. "Ouch!" she cried, bending down to look. Misha saw Avramik glance at Keren in amazement, then run to the riverbank and begin throwing stones in a frenzy.

"That does it!" Misha thought. "All I needed was for Avramik to get into a rock fight with some Arabs."

More stones fell among the children, and there was no telling how it would have ended had it not been for the sudden blast of a horn in the distance. First one long, stubborn beep, then several short, rhythmic ones, like a signal. Turning, they saw the green pickup truck on the ridge behind them.

"What's the pickup doing here?" asked Misha in the sudden silence.

"It's not honking for the fun of it," said Alona in a

choked voice. "Whoever it is, they're looking for us. They're trying to tell us something!"

Misha seized the opportunity. "Let's go," he called, knowing he would be obeyed this time. "Run to the truck, quickly. Alona, make sure no one's left behind!" And he was off like a shot.

Before the children knew it, they were all running after Misha, scrambling up the embankment of the fish ponds and heading for the dirt road. A last barrage of stones fell far behind them. Above them the pickup truck gave a lurch and began quickly zigzagging down, stopping at the bottom to pick up the first of the children. Ovadia, Naomi's father, jumped out of the cabin.

"Climb up quickly," he urged the children. "Onto the truck, all of you!"

Misha, who had slowed down to help Alona with the stragglers, called out, "What is it, Ovadia? What's happening?"

"There's an order to bring all the children back. No one's to be out in the fields who doesn't have to be there!"

"But why? Did something happen on the kibbutz?"

Ovadia was pale. "No, nothing," he said. He waited for Misha to some nearer and added in a low voice, "We got a message from Tel Aviv. A band of Arabs attacked a Jewish bus on its way from Netanya to Jerusalem."

"Was anyone hurt?"

"Yes. Five Jews were killed. And there were wounded, too."

Alona stopped in her tracks and laid a hand on her heart. "This is it," she said in a whisper. "The war's begun."

13

From that day on, nothing was the same. It was no longer possible to go out to the fields without a good reason, and looking for poppies or anemones peeking from beneath rocks was not considered to be one — not as long as there was tension and fighting. Between one house and the next, long communications trenches were dug, crisscrossing the kibbutz with ditches. The old shelters, forgotten after World War II, were cleaned out and made ready.

It was hard to believe the news coming over the radio. Armed bands of Arabs were attacking Jewish buses, neighborhoods, and settlements. Large quantities of weapons and thousands of volunteers were flowing in from neighboring Arab countries to do battle with the Jews.

Yet in the Jordan Valley all was quiet. While the grown-ups secretly cleaned the few guns they had managed to hide from the British and cast a worried eye at the feverish activity in the Arab villages beyond the Yarmuk, the kibbutz turned into a giant amusement park for the children. There was no end of places to explore, of obstacle courses to negotiate, of ditches to jump over or crawl into during a game of hide-and-seek. Every day had its surprises.

One wintry Saturday, when the rain was beating down in torrents on the tile roof of the children's house and endlessly chanting "Sleep! Sleep! Sleep!" to the fourth-graders drowsing beneath their warm blankets, the front door suddenly opened. A pair of heavy boots were wiped clean of mud and pulled off with a thud. Then stockinged feet strode down the hallway between the bedrooms.

"Only Misha walks like that," thought Avramik, opening his eyes. And indeed, at that moment Misha looked in and said, "Good morning, Avramik. Good morning, kids."

"Good morning," mumbled Avramik, raising his head. "Is something up?"

"You bet," answered Misha. "I'm your housemother today."

"No, honest," said Avramik, gripping the corner of his blanket. "Has anything . . . bad . . . happened?"

Misha sat down on the bed and laid a hand on the boy's shoulder. "Not unless it's my being here." He laughed. "It's very simple. At the last kibbutz meeting we voted to go back to the old system we had when you were in first and second grade."

"What was that?"

"Don't you remember, Avramik? You were already here then. On Saturday mornings we grown-ups will take turns being with you until you've all gotten up, made your beds, and gone to your parents' rooms."

"But why go back to that? We're in fourth grade now."

"Why? So as not to leave you all by yourselves. Any objections?"

"None at all," said Avramik. "Not as long as the grown-up is you!"

Misha laughed.

"Hi, Dad, good morning," Rami sang out from the next room. "Where are you? Come say hello!"

Rami's voice woke the others.

"Did you hear that?" asked Shai in the last room. "The grown-ups have started Saturday duty again."

"And today is Rami's father's turn." Brochi rejoiced.

"Great! I always liked Misha's turn best of all."

"Because he tells such good stories."

"Because his stories are the scariest!"

Misha had barely sat down on Rami's bed in Room 3 when the children's house began to stir strangely. Bare feet pattered up and down the hallway and there were whispers and stifled giggles.

"Hey, what's going on?" asked Misha, a mischievous glint in his eyes. "Who are all these ghosts? Where did they come from?"

Bulky figures in white, walking winter blankets, began to appear from the hallway.

His round face peering out from the first blanket, Brochi stopped by Naomi's bed. "Wake up," he ordered. "Sleepy time is over. Sit up and make room."

Avramik, who came after him, hesitated by Rami's

bed. Rina sat up and saw him. "Come sit here, Avramik," she said. "There's plenty of room."

Avramik sat down with his back to the wall, his bare feet curled beneath his blanket.

Misha teased them. "I thought you all wanted to sleep. What's there to get up for on a rainy Saturday morning like this?"

"Nothing," said Ehud, jutting out his jaw, "except to listen to stories."

"It's no use, Misha," Keren said. "You'll just have to tell us a Saturday story the way you used to when we were little."

Misha looked about. All the fourth-graders were seated on the beds, their heads sticking oddly out of their blankets as though they were cherubs swaddled in white clouds.

"Do you remember the adventure we had back in November?" Misha asked, grinning.

"You mean down by the Yarmuk?"

"Yes. It made you good and mad, didn't it?"

"It sure did," said Keren. "I was hit in the leg. It was sore for days after. Why did they do it, Misha? Why do they want to get rid of us? We were born here. This is our home!"

"Why? Simple. The Arabs think this whole country belongs to them. They don't want to share it with us."

"But Misha," Ehud asked, "aren't we still going to have our own state?"

"You bet," said Misha. "But it won't be easy. We're going to have to fight for it. As a matter of fact, we are already fighting for it, even if here in the Jordan Valley things are luckily still quiet."

Rami tugged at his father's sleeve. "Dad, how come those Arab boys who threw stones at us had such good aim? Why did they throw so much better than we did?"

Misha stroked Rami's hair. "Because they're out herding their sheep from the time they're little. Stones are practically the only tools they have. If a sheep strays too far, or a jackal comes too near, they throw a stone at it. That's how they guard their flock. They've had lots of practice, that's all."

"It made me so mad that we couldn't reach them. Not one of us could get a stone across the river. From now on, I'm going to practice, too. I'll throw stones better than any of them."

"Never mind, son," said Misha, putting a big hand on Rami's knee. "I'd rather live with them like good neighbors. In the village of Adassiya, for example, up in the Gilead Mountains, we have friends I wouldn't want to lose. It's too bad you let yourselves get dragged into it."

"We couldn't help it. It got our goat."

"Yes, I realize that," Misha said. "The same thing happened to me once. But then I had a special weapon with me."

"What was it? A pistol? A rifle?"

"What pistol or rifle? The British didn't allow us to carry arms. It was —"

"Maya!" Rami cried happily. "Your boxer, Maya, right?"

"Right. I had Maya."

"Tell us what happened, Dad," Rami begged.

"I'll be glad to. I could talk about Maya all day."

"Then it's about time you did," Giyora exclaimed. "I thought we'd never get around to that story you promised us."

14

"Not so long ago," Misha began, "about the time that you were born —"

Shai interrupted him. "But that *is* long ago. It's nine whole years."

"Well now, that depends on your point of view." Misha smiled. "But all right, Shai, I'll take it back. Long ago, a few months after World War Two began, we felt that something was up in the Arab villages around us. Do you know the feeling of a lull before a storm? Everything is so quiet but so electric that you almost want whatever it is to happen already."

"Right," said Rami. "You feel as if you're going to explode."

"Exactly. There was so much tension in the air that we didn't know which was better, to go on waiting or to have the storm break, even if it was a bad one. And do you know who helped me keep calm then?"

"Mira, Rami's mother," said Naomi.

Misha laughed. "Yes, she did, too. But there was someone else, someone named —"

"Maya!" exclaimed Rami again. "Your boxer, Maya."

"Right. Maya was the best watchdog I ever had, and believe me, I've raised some pretty good ones. She was long-legged and wiry with a well-shaped head, and she always looked alert."

"I think boxers are ugly," Keren said. "They look so mean and ugly."

"You're thinking of bulldogs." Rami scoffed. "They really do look like mean old men. Boxers are something else. They're much better-looking and smarter."

Giyora was annoyed. "Why don't you stop interrupting Misha. We want to listen to a story, not to some silly argument about boxers and bulldogs."

"From now on, no more comments from the audience," said Misha. "Okay?"

"Okay!" chorused the children, quieting down, at least for a while.

Misha continued. "One day, about Passover time, when we were having the first heat wave of the spring, I was working on the combine in the tractor shed. Our kibbutz was still in its old location, down near the Jordan, and from the shed you could see the dirt road that wound up from the river to our gate. You *could* see it, but I didn't, because my head was in the engine of the tractor. I was looking for a screw that had fallen into the transmission. Maya was dozing nearby, knocked out by the heat, I guess. Suddenly she growled. All at once she was wide awake, and before I could even straighten up she was standing on all fours and quivering like a taut spring, staring at a point on the road between us and the Jordan.

"I turned to look, and right away I knew what it was. The storm had broken. Eliahu was running toward me, waving his arms and shouting something that I couldn't understand. I began running toward him with Maya at my side. Every now and then she'd slow down, look around, and then catch up again. Eliahu was pale and covered with dust, and so out of breath that he could hardly get a word out.

" 'Ovadia . . . down there . . . with the sheep . . . attacked by Arabs —'

" 'Where?' I asked. 'Exactly where is he?'

" 'On the little island in the Jordan.' Eliahu panted.

" 'Alone?'

" 'Yes. With the flock. The Arabs from the village marched on our vineyard and new orange grove. They cut him off from the kibbutz, so he headed for the island.'

"Now I had a clear picture. That winter, the Jordan had flooded and short-cut one of its own bends. The high ground of the bend had become a little island, but the water between it and the bank was shallow and could be crossed easily by the sheep. That's where they and Ovadia had taken cover.

"Maya stood tensely, letting out low growls. I took her chain from my pocket and clipped it to her choke. I knew what that tension meant in her and didn't want to release it too soon.

" 'Go for help!' I told Eliahu. 'I'm heading down to the Jordan.'

"Down the hill, on a hidden part of the slope, I could hear loud shouts in Arabic. There were curses, threats, and bursts of laughter. Maya lunged, pulling me after her with the chain held tight in my hand. As soon as we came to the edge of the hill I saw everything. The vineyard below was swarming with people. The whole Arab village was there, their dark clothes standing out against the green of the grapevines. A large band of boys was busy uprooting the saplings in the new orange grove nearby. Everyone else was looking at the sheep huddled on the island in the Jordan. Ovadia was standing in the middle of them."

"I know this story," declared Naomi, Ovadia's daughter. "My father once told it to me."

The other children hushed her. "Be quiet! We promised Misha not to interrupt until he was finished."

Naomi persisted. "But I know what the Arabs did. They threw stones, just like those boys by the Yarmuk."

"That's right," said Misha. "They threw stones at Ovadia. They did it as though it was a game, throwing a stone and laughing, throwing again and cursing. But it wasn't a game for Ovadia. The stones were coming closer and closer. He kept trying to dodge, hiding behind the sheep while protecting his head with his hands.

"Maya kept tugging at the chain, her breath coming in quick pants. Down by the riverbank I saw an Arab whom I recognized. He was one of the village toughs, a great big fellow with a violent temper. He stuck out head and shoulders above the mob, and I could see by

76

the way he shouted the loudest and threw the most stones that he was its leader.

"I bent down close to Maya. 'At him, girl!' I told her. 'Get that one over there!' I pointed to the leader.

"I don't know if she really understood me or if it was just her canine sixth sense that told her whom to get in that mob, but she never took her eyes off him as I slipped the chain off her choke. 'It's up to you now, Maya,' I whispered. And freeing her, I shouted, 'Go!'

"Maya streaked down the slope like a whirlwind. She didn't bark once. She didn't make a sound. She flashed through the mob like an arrow, making straight for the big Arab. The two of them vanished in a cloud of dust. For a minute I couldn't see her at all. I guess the mob could, though, because it panicked. Everyone began running every which way, screaming as though for dear life. Before long, the vineyard was deserted. So was the ruined orange grove. Only one man was lying by the dusty road. It was the leader of the mob, of course, and Maya was standing over him with her head down, her legs dug in and spread wide. I could see that she had a hold on him, but where? I found out when I came running up to them. Maya's teeth were in the man's chest, pinning him to the ground. It was all I could do to make her let go.

"I bent down over him. His dark face was twisted with pain. '*Min wayn inte?*' I asked in Arabic. 'Where are you from?'

"He didn't answer me.

" 'What's your name?'

77

"He gave me a quick glance, then turned his head away. I'll never forget that look. It was full of scorn and terrible hatred. The boys who threw stones at us down by the Yarmuk made me think of it. And both times I felt sad. It wasn't the way I'd imagined being neighbors with the Arabs. I'd had other dreams. Of friendship, of trust, of mutual respect . . ."

"And that's all?" asked Avramik. "That's the end of the story?"

"No," said Misha. "Not exactly. We brought the fellow to the hospital and thought it was the end of the story, too. But it wasn't. The next day the British police turned up at the kibbutz and demanded 'the wild beast.' That's what they called Maya."

"And you let them have her?"

"What do you think?" asked Misha, his eyes flashing mischievously. "That I'd give them Maya?"

"But what did you do?"

"Well, I couldn't refuse them, could I? As long as they were the government, I was duty-bound to obey. Or to seem to, anyway."

"Misha, you're keeping us in suspense," said Keren. "What did you do with Maya?"

"Simple," said Misha. "There was a stray dog who used to hang around the kibbutz, looking for food. We put a collar on it and gave it to the British."

"And they really believed it was Maya?"

"I can't say for a fact if they did or not, but I know the Arabs didn't."

"How?" asked Rina.

Misha grinned. "That's another story!"

15

It was pouring. The sodden branches of the olive trees lashed at the walls, at the roof, at the windows of the children's house.

Misha watched the rain run down a window pane. "I do believe that this will go down in history as the rainiest Saturday of 1948," he said with a smile.

"I like it," said Keren. "We can't go to our parents in a flood like this, anyway, so you can tell us another story about Maya, can't you, Misha?"

"But what do you care about things that happened when you were still wet behind the ears?" Misha asked with a straight face.

"Dad, will you stop it," said Rami. "Can't you see we're all dying of curiosity?"

Misha looked around him. The fourth-graders were sitting on the edge of their beds, hanging on his every word. "All right," he said, giving in. "I'll tell you the rest of it. I've already told you that the Arabs weren't fooled. They knew the dog we gave the British was just an ordinary animal, and they were waiting for a chance to get even.

"The worst time of the year was always the summer harvest. That's when we and the Arabs had the biggest

79

run-ins. As soon as our wheat was ready to reap, they would go down to our fields with their sickles and cut as much as they could. No matter how quickly we drove them off, they always managed to get away with some of the crop. And sometimes they'd drive their flocks through the rest of it and ruin it entirely, just out of spite.

"Before the harvest, then, we were always on guard. We made sure that someone was always in the fields, ready to run for help at the first sign of trouble.

"One afternoon I went down to the wheat field. As usual, I took Maya, on a chain. From a distance I could see there was already someone in the field. 'Here we go again,' I thought. 'They're stealing our wheat this year, too.' But while they usually started cutting along the edges of the field so that they could slip away in time, this time they had started in the middle. I supposed they must have thought it would keep them from being seen. Well, they were wrong.

"I laid my hand on Maya's head — that was our signal to be quiet — and headed on down to the field. To my surprise, there were only two reapers in it, a woman and a boy. They had their backs turned and didn't notice me. The woman was cutting the wheat quickly with a small sickle, and the boy was binding it in little sheaves. Maya was bristling all over, but I wasn't going to turn her loose. Women and children weren't my idea of fair game. I knew that all I had to do was scold them and give them a warning. I kept Maya on a tight leash, though she kept turning this way and that and tugging at the chain.

"I was near the two reapers when the earth suddenly seemed to open around me. A circle of Arabs rose out of the wheat, surrounding me on all sides. The woman and boy took off and were gone, and there I was by myself, smack in the middle of a trap. That is, there *we* were — Maya and I.

"I wasn't armed. I stood there facing them with only my bare hands and thought, 'I'm a goner!'

"This time they didn't use stones. They all had heavy clubs, *nabuts*, they call them in Arabic. Slowly the circle began closing in on me. I couldn't make out any faces. They were hidden by the kaffiyehs the men wore, so that all you could see was their eyes, gleaming with confidence that their quarry lay helpless before them.

"Maya was running in little circles around me, held tight by her choke. I whipped the chain off her and she sprang forward, lunging at the nearest man. The Arabs raised their clubs and shouted, trying to get a swing at her. She kept running in circles, charging forward and darting back to stay out of reach of the clubs whistling through the air. Whichever way she turned, though, there were more of them. The whole thing seemed planned more for her benefit than for mine. Meanwhile, I kept looking for an opening in the circle of men, backing up slowly as I did, until — wham! — I had fallen into a pit I hadn't known was there. 'This is it,' I told myself. 'They've got me now.'

"Then I heard Maya barking furiously. A moment later she was looking down at me from the top of the pit. 'Maya!' I yelled. 'Run for it! Run back to the kibbutz! Run!'

"I don't know if dogs understand our language, but I do know one thing: Maya understood me as perfectly as if I had spoken hers. She hurdled the pit with a leap. I heard shouts of surprise that soon turned to disappointed curses. I knew right away what that meant: Maya was safe. She had broken through the circle and gotten away. For a moment I felt as happy as if I had managed to run back through the fields to the kibbutz myself, but a shower of earth on my head soon brought me back to reality. I was trapped, helpless and alone.

"A shadow fell on me. I looked up to see a wall of men ringing the pit and hiding the light of the sun. A foot kicked more dirt down on me and somebody laughed. Another foot nudged a large clod of earth into the pit, and someone else stamped at the edge of it. Then I knew: they were going to bury me alive, slowly, as though it was a game, for the fun of it. I was scared out of my wits. I started screaming like a madman. And the strange thing was, it wasn't something I had meant to do; it was as if someone else was inside me, shrieking his head off. Pretty soon the feet at the top of the pit stopped their kicking. The shadows of the men disappeared. '*Majnun!*' I heard one of them say in amazement.

"Yes, I was *majnun*. Crazy, as crazy as a loon! I kept screaming and shouting and yelling like a lunatic, and all that time the word *majnun* kept raining down on me, echoing through my head, coming at me from all sides.

"When my throat was too dry to scream any longer I slumped to the ground and looked up. There was no one there. The Arabs had all gone. They had decided I was crazy, and a crazy man, according to their code, is an untouchable."

Misha broke off his story and glanced about the room. The fourth-graders sat on pins and needles, waiting with sparkling eyes to hear the rest. Then his glance fell on Avramik. The boy crouched on Rina's bed as though paralyzed, the life drained from his body.

"What's wrong, Avramik? You look pale."

"I never knew that . . . that you came that close to . . . not being here. How did you ever get out of there?"

"Well, it's a fact that I am here, isn't it?" Misha said, grinning.

"Yes, but they almost killed you."

Misha rose and went to sit by Avramik. "Listen to the end of it," he said, putting his long arm around the boy's shoulder. "I have no idea how long I sat in that pit. I think I must have blacked out for a while. When I came to I heard Maya barking and some people calling. At first I didn't know who they were. One shouted something I couldn't make out and the other yelled, 'Abu-Rami!' The Arabs call a father by the name of his eldest son, and there was only one person who ever called me that. 'It can't be,' I thought. 'I must be dreaming or the devil knows what.' But the barks kept coming closer and then I saw Maya's head, a dark shadow against the blue sky. On her heels came two men who knelt and looked down at me. I couldn't make out their faces.

" 'Hey, are you all right?' one of them called down.

"I didn't recognize him.

"'Abu-Rami?' the other called in a deep voice. 'Is that you? Are you alive?'

"'Abu-Musa, it's you,' I called back.

"Yes, it was Abu-Musa from the Baha'i village of Adassiya. We were old friends. He took to calling me that when you were born, Rami. He did business with Jews and spoke good Hebrew."

"And he got you out of the pit?"

"Yes. They threw down a rope for me. You should have seen Maya dance for joy. She jumped all over me, licked my face, whined, barked, licked me some more. She was so excited that she almost knocked me back into the pit."

"But Misha," Keren asked, "who was the other man?"

"The other man was Yankeleh from Yavne'el. He and Abu-Musa were involved in some business deal and happened to be driving down the road, not far from the field. Maya saw him through the windshield of the car and recognized him. He recognized her, too. And as for the rest of it, I've already told you."

Rami stretched his legs beneath his blanket. "And didn't you give Abu-Musa Maya's puppy, Dad?"

"Yes. Maya gave birth to two pups a few months afterward, a male and a female. I gave the male to Abu-Musa and the female to Yankeleh. I thought that was the best way to thank them."

"They were pedigreed boxers, weren't they?"

"They were. Had I known they would be Maya's last pups, I would never have given them away . . . No, I guess I would have anyway. Why, those two men

84

saved my life! And besides, Yankeleh breeds his dog and has fine puppies from her every year. We're good friends and I can always ask him for a pup that will look just like Grandmother Maya."

The sky was clearing. A Sabbath sun shone down on the kibbutz. Wisps of vapor curled over the paths and droplets sparkled on the wet leaves like jewels.

"All's well that ends well," Misha concluded. "The story's over, so is the rain, and now it's time for you to get dressed and hightail it to your parents, do you hear?"

Before anyone could move, though, there was a quick bark outside. The door opened and in stepped a lively brown boxer who began to sniff at all the children. Misha jumped up, staring at it.

"Abu-Musa!" he exclaimed. "Abu-Musa's here in the kibbutz."

16

When Naomi was a little girl — a really little girl, not just the shortest fourth-grader — she thought her father had two faces. One was his "Daddy" face, which was smiling, joking, and always gay. The other was his "Civil Defense Chief" face, which was stern, serious, and always worrying about the kibbutz.

That late winter day of 1948, when her father stood in the doorway of the children's house with the man called Abu-Musa, Naomi thought of those two faces. She knew right away that, as far as her father was concerned, it was a "lost Saturday": the stern, serious man in the doorway was Ovadia the Civil Defense Chief. It was obvious that Naomi, her mother, and her sister would have to spend the day without him and that he would even miss the "Hebrew Hit Parade," his favorite radio program.

Rami, however, was not about to relinquish his father so easily. When his mother took Arnon out for a walk and he and Avramik were asked to leave his parents' room, he did not go very far. The room drew him like a magnet. Why had Abu-Musa suddenly appeared? What had he come to tell his father and Ovadia? It was clearly some sort of secret, because otherwise they all wouldn't have had to leave the room.

Rami stood at the rear of the house, his back against the wall. Inching along like a crab, he took a step with his left foot, brought his right foot up to it, and stepped again with his left. The leaves of the pipal tree shed large, cold drops of water on his head, the last of the rain that had fallen on the Valley that morning.

"It's a good thing it rained," Rami thought. "If the leaves on the ground were dry, I'd make more noise." Silently, he glided along the wall.

There was a sound to his right. Turning quickly, he saw Avramik standing there, his eyes narrowed and his lips pursed determinedly.

"Good grief," thought Rami. "He's a regular tail.

There's no getting rid of him." And in a whisper he said, "Beat it! Who invited you?"

"I want to hear what they're saying, too," Avramik answered. "What makes you think you're the only one?"

"Shhh, quiet!" Rami hissed in alarm. "They'll hear us."

"So what?" retorted Avramik. "I have as much right to be here as you do."

The muffled men's voices coming from inside fell silent for a moment. Rami held his breath. "All I need," he thought, "is for them to find me eavesdropping."

But Abu-Musa was again talking in low tones.

"What a stubborn ass you are," Rami whispered. Yet he had no choice. "All right," he said. "Just keep your mouth shut, okay?"

Avramik didn't answer. He leaned his back against the wall and extended a foot to his left. Rami shrugged. There was nothing he could do about it. Carefully he began to inch along the wall again until he was under the window.

"Don't think it's over," Abu-Musa was saying. "If you ask me, it's just beginning."

Ovadia could be heard clearly. "But ever since the attack on Tirat Tsevi was thrown back, the Valley has been quiet."

"It won't stay that way for long," said Abu-Musa in his deep, guttural voice. "All the Arab villages are full of . . . What's the word in Hebrew?"

"Volunteers?"

"Yes, volunteers. They call themselves the Arab

Army of Salvation. Syrian and Iraqi officers are training them, and so are some Englishmen who've run away from the British army."

"Deserters," said Misha.

"And the villages here in the Valley, across the river?" Ovadia asked.

"They have a special force of their own called the Yarmuk Brigade."

"What do you think will happen?" asked Misha.

"It can only get worse. Much worse. They're waiting for the day your state is officially declared. What you've seen so far will seem like child's play then."

"What do you mean?"

"Look," Abu-Musa explained, "until now you've only been fighting the local Palestinian Arabs reinforced by a few volunteers, as you call them. But the minute a Jewish state is declared, you'll have a real war on your hands with every Arab country in the area: Syria, Transjordan, Iraq, Lebanon, even Egypt. That's right, Egypt too. They'll all move on you together, and then —"

A dry branch crackled beneath Rami's foot. The voices in the room fell silent again. Rami anxiously flattened himself against the wall, feeling Avramik's mocking eyes. His face turned so red that the freckles dotting it disappeared. Someone came to the window, looked out, and sat down again. The three men resumed their conversation, in still lower tones than before. Only bits and snatches of it could be heard now. The freckles reappeared on Rami's face.

"And you? Your family?"

Abu-Musa murmured something indistinct.

"We'll think of something," said Misha. "You musn't stay in your village, in any case. It's too dangerous."

"What? Secretly, of course, what else?"

"There are others? I thought there were."

"It isn't easy," said Abu-Musa, his voice clearer now. "The Baha'is in our village came from Persia many years ago. We were persecuted there because our religion is different from that of the Moslems. Here we've been much better off. Our lives have been quiet and there's enough water from the Yarmuk to grow all the fruit trees and vegetables we want. I swear, it's a paradise. And now we'll have to leave it all again."

"Let's hope it's only temporarily," said Ovadia.

"You say you have family in Haifa? In Acre? Uncles and cousins? That's good. What you should do is . . ."

The voices grew lower again, like a gust of wind retreating into the mountains.

On the far side of the house a door opened. The men seemed to have finished talking. "Hey, Rami," Misha called.

Rami flew around the house. "Yes, Dad, what is it?"

"Do you have any idea where Mom put the sugar? I want to make some coffee."

"Tea for me," said Abu-Musa in his deep voice. "Strong, sweet tea. Have you forgotten, Abu-Rami? It really has been a long time."

Rami found the sugar at once. He had a sweet tooth and always knew where such things were. Sitting off to the side, he watched the three men silently sipping their hot drinks. Vaguely he could sense the things that bound them: old friendship, the feeling of shared danger, and the confidence that they could trust each other. Yet he himself was not part of it. He was just a boy who didn't belong with the grown-ups. Even Misha, his father, seemed suddenly a stranger from whose world Rami was excluded.

"I've got to think of something," Rami said to himself. He had to think of something that would be just his, just the children's, that would give their lives, too, meaning and a sense of common purpose.

Suddenly he chuckled out loud, causing Avramik to look at him in surprise. Rami's eyes gleamed. He had it, and what an idea it was! But he was not going to tell Avramik now. Why give him the pleasure? He would wait for the chance that would make him, Rami, the king of the class.

17

They were all perched on top of the air-raid shelter during recess. Though the shelter had been cleaned and made ready for emergencies, it looked the same as always from the outside, like the hulk of some large hibernating animal that was dead to the world and to all the commotion around it. Thick grass dotted with yellow dandelions overgrew it.

The group of boys and girls on the shelter had no leader. When you grew up with the same children in one house, sat next to them at every meal, went to one kindergarten with them and afterward to one school, it was hard to take orders from any of them. Why should you? Who was anyone to order you around? What made one child better than another?

Hard, but not impossible, because today Rami was their leader. There was no doubt about it, the idea was his.

"My dad says it's okay," Rami said, his eyes shining. "He'll get us the puppy."

"But what will we do with it?" Keren asked.

"We'll train it. It'll be our class watchdog."

"But the kibbutz is guarded already." Naomi objected, raising her eyebrows.

"Oof," Rami exclaimed impatiently. "So what if it is? With an attack dog of our own we can go anywhere we want. We can even spy on the Arab villages without anyone throwing stones at us."

Avramik stood off to one side as if in a world of his own. But then he said to Rami, "That's what you think. Big deal! If they throw stones at you from across the river, do you think an attack dog's going to help? The only way to stand up to them is to learn to throw better than they do, and that's a fact."

By way of illustration he picked up a stone and fired it into some distant rose bushes.

"Not bad," said Ehud admiringly. "You've been practicing, huh?"

Avramik didn't answer. He just stuck his hands in his pockets and turned his back.

"Listen," said Rami, trying to change the subject back again. "My dad told me that Lilith, Maya's daughter, had pups a few weeks ago."

"Where, in Yavne'el?"

"Yes, at his friend Yankeleh's. If we all chip in, we can buy one. I tell you, it'll be a real boxer, just like Maya: strong, smart, and loyal. We'll do super things with it."

"You bet! It'll be the class dog. Whoever chips in will go partners, okay?"

"It's fine with me," said Ehud. "I have a whole British pound sterling. My uncle in Tel Aviv sent it to me for my birthday. I'll use it to buy a share in the puppy."

"Great idea," said Ofra enthusiastically. "I have a little money, too."

"A little?"

"Yes . . ." She was embarrassed. "A few cents."

"So what if it's just a few cents?" Rami asked in an unexpected burst of generosity. "If we all give a little, there'll be enough."

Naomi stared uncomfortably at the ground. "But I don't have any money at all," she said with a blush. "Not even a few cents."

"Didn't you get anything for your birthday?" asked Rami.

"Only a new book and a silver chain with a medal of Jerusalem."

"Fine," said Rami. "We'll sell it. I'm sure you can sell that kind of thing in Tiberias."

His eyes fell on Avramik, whose back was still turned. There was a new glint in Rami's eyes, the unspoken germ of an idea. Avramik shifted from foot to foot, his hands still in his pockets. It was difficult to tell if he was listening.

"Hey, Avramik," Rami called, lingering over every word. "You can have a share in the puppy, too. All you have to do is give us your chain with the Star of David."

Avramik froze. They all held their breaths. Since the day of his arrival in the kibbutz, no one had dared mention his chain to him. He had brought it with him from "over there," from the Europe of World War II, and it was not a subject one could raise with him. For that matter, it was not a subject one could raise with anyone.

Not unless you were Rami. "What's the matter?" he taunted. "Can't bear to part with it? You don't want to stop looking like a girl?"

"Shut up!" said Rina. "Why don't you just shut up, Rami!"

"Just who do you think *you* are?" Rami inquired in a loud voice.

"Yeah, who asked you anyway?" put in Giyora, who hadn't forgotten Rina's joke. The bottom of the barrel, she had called him, because he always took what was left. Now was his chance to get back at her. "Maybe that chain was a present you gave him, eh?"

Rina gulped. If only she could stop them. If only she could make the two of them shut their mouths.

But Rami, egged on by Giyora, was already asking, in a voice as sweet as pie, "You want to go partners in our puppy, Avramik?"

"I don't like dogs," said Avramik, his back still turned.

"What do you like," teased Rami, "girls' jewelry?"

"Yeah, and keeping food beneath his bed," added Giyora.

Avramik spun around. His face was pale, his eyes narrowed into thin, hostile slits. The box beneath his bed was another taboo topic.

Rina jumped up. "Giyora, that's enough. I'm warning you!"

"Oh, you are? And just what do you plan on doing to me, big shot?"

"Hey, you gave me an idea," said Rami. "We'll sell Avramik's box. We'll finally find out what's in there!"

"Dresses to wear with his jewelry, I'll bet," said Giyora. "Besides all that bread, of course."

Giyora felt confident beside Rami, who had shot up and was now the tallest boy in the class, and the best Indian wrestler, too.

With Giyora sticking to him like a shadow, Rami sauntered over to Avramik. "So tell us," he asked, "whom are you keeping that chain for?"

"I'll bet it's for his sweetheart, Rina," said Giyora.

They stood facing Avramik. Rami felt that nothing

could stop him now, that nothing could stand in his way. He had had that feeling once before, and he knew that in another minute he would say something unforgivable, something he could never take back. The feeling was overpowering, like a wave. He reached out and grabbed the Star of David. "What's the matter?" he taunted, feeling the wave crest and break. "Are you keeping it for your mama? Well, your mama won't be coming, little boy!"

Avramik's face was distorted by pain. For a moment his knees seemed to buckle; then he struck at Rami's outstretched hand, turned, and dashed down the slope of the shelter. He was gone in a second.

Rina bolted after him. She saw him pass the last row of houses, jump over a communications trench, race by the chicken coops, and head for the front gate of the kibbutz. She ran as fast as her legs could carry her, waving to the guard to stop him, but Avramik was past the gate and into a field of clover. Rina had to slow down.

"Hey, Avramik," the guard called, "you're not allowed past the gate!"

"I'll get him," Rina shouted, passing the gate herself. "Don't chase him. I'll bring him back."

But Avramik was already far ahead of her, a small black dot in a field of green clover.

18

At the far end of the clover was a stand of young bananas. The small shoots stood in rows that seemed too big for them. One of them appeared to be moving in the distance. It was Avramik, still running.

"Avramik!" cried Rina. "Avramik, wait for me."

But the distant figure didn't stop. Rina's breath came in gasps. She slowed down and looked around. She was in a place she had never been before. Their class had never come here, which was strange because it was a lovely spot. Beyond the bananas was a small wheat field, and still farther, a catchment pond, the reservoir of the kibbutz. On the dirt embankment that circled it grew a thick line of huge eucalyptus trees, looking like giant eyelashes against the bright green of the fields.

Avramik was heading straight toward the pond. What was he going to do there? "Avramik!" she called again, cupping her hands to her mouth. "Wait up, do you hear me? Wait!"

Avramik stopped for a second, turned around to look, and started to run again. He passed the last row of bananas, crossed the path dividing them from the wheat field, and entered the wheat. He was no longer running, but she couldn't tell if it was because he was tired or because the wheat was too thick. She knew only that she had a stitch in her side and couldn't run another step.

Rina walked through the banana stand, keeping her eye on Avramik crossing the wheat field, his head and shoulders bobbing above the stalks. A breeze rippled the velvety green grain. Like a small boat making for an island, Avramik forged steadily ahead.

Banks of pale yellow wild mustard and bright yellow chrysanthemums flowered between the field and the path. It was full spring. The intoxicating scent of the flowers and the buzzing of thousands of bees assailed her from all sides.

She paused for a moment, then cut through the bank of spring flowers into the wheat field. Oddly, the buzzing of the bees grew even louder. Ahead of her Avramik was nearing the pond. In another minute he would reach the embankment.

And then it dawned on Rina why the children were never brought to this spot. Under the eucalyptuses on the embankment stood dozens of wooden boxes painted blue: bee hives!

And Avramik was so close to them. A few more steps and —

Rina wanted to run to him, to shout at the top of her lungs, but it was too late. Far off she saw Avramik wave first one hand, then another, then slap at himself. He screamed. Striking out wildly, he began to run. He fell, picked himself up, ran some more, and fell again.

The tranquil, steady buzzing that came from all around turned into a menacing drone. The bees were pouring out of their boxes, on the warpath!

Rina threw herself face-down among the wheat stalks. "Be still," she told herself. "Be still! Don't move! Don't stick out! Don't let them see you!"

She had once been told that the worst thing to do with bees was make them angry. "Be quiet, Rina, even if you're bitten! Control yourself! Don't slap! Don't panic!"

A cloud of furious bees swept overhead, swirled searchingly in wide circles, and flew on. Rina covered her ears and buried her face in the ground. Right next to her a silky pink flax flower was peacefully blooming, its petals turned in rapture toward the sun. If only she, too, were a flower, peaceful in the field.

"I've got to get back," she thought feverishly. "I've got to! The beekeeper will know what to do. Someone will know. I've got to save Avramik!"

The angry drone of the hives came from farther away now, as if on a different trail, though many bees still buzzed above the wheat stalks.

Slowly, quietly, Rina began crawling through the wheat. "Easy does it! No quick movements, remember!" She passed a purple gladiolus tall among the stalks, hardly noticing it, though there were times she would have gone out of her way to find it. She crawled on. Finally she was at the edge of the field, by the bank of wildflowers. Bees flitted busily among the chrysanthemums and wild mustard, once more buzzing tranquilly. The world was its old self again, a place where bees stuck to flowers and to making honey for the kibbutz.

Still crawling, Rina crossed the bank of flowers. She was on the open road leading back to the kibbutz, unprotected and exposed. But she had no choice. She had to get up. Little by little. First on all fours, next on her knees, and then on her feet. She stood still for a moment, listening, and then began to walk, slowly at first and then faster. Was the danger over? The drone of the bees was far away, almost inaudible. She turned around to look back at the wheat field. Avramik was nowhere to be seen. The waves of green grain had capsized the little boat.

With the last of her strength, Rina began to run. She crossed the banana stand with its sea of small saplings, stumbling in the soft earth.

In the distance, by the front gate of the kibbutz, she saw a crowd of people. Something must have happened. A Jeep drove up to the gate and screeched to a halt. God, give her the strength to get there! Give her the strength to tell them what had happened, to lead them back to Avramik!

19

An uncomfortable silence had descended on the children when Avramik and Rina disappeared. Rami stood pale-faced, his eyes on the ground. The others, aghast, all moved away from him. Only Giyora wavered, shuffling his feet as if trying to make up his mind about something important. At last he turned his back to Rami and climbed down from the shelter, too.

"What's wrong with you all?" Rami challenged. "What do you want from me?"

No one answered.

"If the whole class decided to buy a puppy, shouldn't he have chipped in, too?"

"What for?" asked Keren. "He doesn't owe you anything. If he didn't want to go partners, he didn't have to."

"But he's always doing annoying things like that. Ever since the first day he came here," Rami argued, his eyes looking for someone to agree with him. No one met his gaze.

"That's not so," said Ehud. "He's just different. So what if he's not like us? You have no idea what he went through."

"Neither do you!" Rami shot back.

"That's right," Ehud agreed. "But his being different doesn't annoy me. You're jealous, that's all."

"Me, jealous? What are you talking about?"

"You bet you are!" exclaimed Naomi. "Everyone knows it's because of how he feels about your father —"

"And how your father feels about him," Shai put in.

"We thought you'd help him adjust," said Keren, "because you were his cousin. But you're the one who caused him the most trouble, right from the start. And besides, you're . . . you're . . ."

"I'm what?" snapped Rami.

Keren hesitated. The thought she'd been about to express felt like a hot coal on her tongue.

Rami was shouting now. "You have to stick your nose into this, too! Why, you don't even sleep in his room. You never did. You never had to see that secret box of his that no one's even allowed to touch."

"He's not in your room anymore."

"Yes, but he was. You don't know what you're talking about. You wouldn't have liked it, either, seeing him with that private box of his when all the rest of us have open shelves that you can't hide a thing on."

Keren moved closer to Ehud, as if for protection. The words on her tongue came tumbling out all at once.

"I want you to know that I saw everything. I saw you try to push Avramik into the fish pond. Ehud and I were behind you and we saw. And you had the nerve to blame him and say it was his fault that you fell. Well, we saw it, didn't we, Ehud?"

"We sure did," Ehud said solemnly. "We were right behind you. I told you even then."

Rami, his mouth opening and shutting, squirmed. He was at a loss for words.

"You kept trying to make him miserable," said Naomi, joining the fray. "From the day your father brought him. And he always tried his best. Sure, it was hard for him, but he never cried once." To Naomi, who cried at the drop of a hat, this was the ultimate compliment.

"You know something?" said Shai, who had been sitting quietly, scuffing the grass with his foot. "Naomi's right. I never once saw him cry. Never. And he had some good reasons to. The only one who ever helped him was Rina."

"That's a fact," said Ehud. "Rina was the only one."

"Cripes, now you're dragging in Rina," said Rami. "I'll bet she's in love with him. I'll bet you anything she is."

"She is not," said Naomi. "She just wanted to be nice. And she is nice. She helped him right from the beginning, even though she has no father —"

"Not 'even though,'" remarked Giyora, who had kept out of it until now. "Because. I'll bet it's because she has no father that . . ."

Rami gave him a quick look. The one person he'd thought he could count on had gone over to the enemy. "You're chicken," he said. "You're just sticking up for Rina because of everyone."

"I am not," answered Giyora, his round face blushing. "I . . . I'm honestly sorry for what I said before. I was mad at her because she once called me . . . Heck, it doesn't matter."

"It does too matter!" Rami insisted. "She called you the fat bottom of the barrel. And you want to know something? She was right. She really was. Just look at yourself."

Giyora turned crimson from ear to ear. He looked like a boiling kettle with a stopped spout, about to burst. At last he spluttered, "If you're . . . as lowdown as that . . . then everyone might as well know that you've been lying all along. We never had to buy that puppy in the first place. Your father said that Yankeleh would let us have it for nothing, that he'd just be returning a gift. There! Now everyone knows."

Giyora took a deep breath. Having let off steam, he was no longer red in the face. On the contrary, he was white as a sheet. So were all the other children surrounding Rami, who stood there staring at the ground.

"All right," he said in a choked voice. "All right . . ."

There was a big lump in his throat, but he musn't cry, not in front of them. He musn't give them the satisfaction.

"All right, I shouldn't have done it. I just . . . I —"

A loud bell interrupted him. Recess was over. The invisible ring around them was gone, too. They began to run back to the classroom.

"Not back to class, you dopes!" Ehud shouted after them. "To the front gate!"

"Ehud's right! To the gate!"

"That's where they went."

"We've got to find Avramik."

"We'll need help. He's probably run away."

Like a flock of birds changing course in midair, the

103

children wheeled toward the gate, leaving Rami all by himself, the lump still in his throat. He'd be darned if he'd cry, though, even if there was no one to see him.

The wind carried his classmates' excited cries to him. Slowly he began to walk after them. His legs felt like lead. With a supreme effort, as though in a nightmare, Rami made himself walk faster toward the crowd at the gate. Beyond the perimeter fence, on the road by the clover, he saw a small figure run, stumble, and run some more. Rina!

The gate swung open wide and the Jeep sped toward her.

"Avramik!" Rina shouted, pointing toward the distant reservoir. "He's there, in the wheat! With lots of bees! Lots!" Exhausted, she collapsed in the middle of the road.

20

Avramik spent several days in the hospital in Tiberias. After a week Misha brought him back to the kibbutz, where he was given a room in the infirmary.

The infirmary was a long, low building that stood in a clump of pine trees. Its rooms opened on a white-walled, well-scrubbed hallway whose floor gleamed from constant mopping.

Some of the kibbutz members liked to joke about the nurse in charge. "In Elka's infirmary you can eat right off the floor!"

"That's assuming you could smuggle food in," others answered. "Just try it and see what happens!"

"You think the problem is just food? Try visiting without permission and she'll raise the roof, too!"

But when Elka took Avramik into her kingdom, putting him between fresh sheets, she had no idea what she was in for. An hour hadn't passed before she was doing battle with the fourth-graders, and by the end of the day she could see that it was a lost cause.

"All right." She shrugged, giving in. "You can come visit, but not too many at once. Two at a time. That's the limit. And make sure you wipe your shoes before entering, do you hear?"

"We hear you."

"And if you see he's tired, you must leave at once. Do you promise?"

"We promise. May we come in now?"

And so the procession began. First they lined up by twos and carefully wiped their shoes. Then they tip-toed down the hallway that smelled of hygiene and medicines and slipped into Avramik's room. Ehud and Keren were the first.

"Well?" asked the others, besieging them when they came out. "How does he look?"

"Awful!" said Keren. "His face is all puffed up."

Ehud corrected her. "It's not as bad as all that. It only seems so because he's so thin. They say that in the hospital they could hardly see his eyes."

"They're like two slits now, too," Keren insisted.

"You're exaggerating!"

"Did he talk to you?"

"A bit . . ."

Ofra carefully donned the wreath of dry pine needles that she had made for herself while waiting. "Did he tell you exactly what happened to him?" she asked. "Why he ran there, of all places?"

"Some chance of that," Ehud answered. "We weren't crazy enough to ask him. I just sat there and told him jokes. He even laughed at one of them, didn't he, Keren?"

"Well, he did smile."

"It's my turn now," Ofra announced. "Who's coming with me?"

"I am," said Naomi, jumping up. Quickly she wiped her feet on the small mat by the door. Suddenly she turned around and asked, "Has anyone seen Rami?"

No one answered.

"Do you think he'll come visit Avramik?"

"I have no idea," said Giyora. "He's hardly said a word since it happened. He just walks around looking blue. I'll bet he's sorry. He feels so bad, he's eating himself up."

"He ought to," said Naomi, resuming wiping her shoes energetically on the mat.

"Naomi," Ofra pleaded, "please give me a chance, too. You'll wipe your soles clean off if you don't stop. And if Elka catches me with dirty shoes, who knows what she'll do? She's liable to give me an anti-dirt injection!"

Naomi was too busy thinking to laugh. "But what if Rami does come?" she asked.

"If he does," said Giyora, "we'll let him go to the head of the line. Don't you think it's awfully important for them to talk to each other?"

But Rami did not come. Misha, on the other hand, spent a long time with Avramik that afternoon.

"How are you feeling today?" he asked, studying Avramik's face.

"Fine" was the terse answer.

"At least you don't look like a purple balloon anymore. You should have seen yourself a few days ago." Misha sat in a white chair by the bed. "How are you getting along with Elka? She doesn't put you in the washing machine twice a day?"

"Only twice? Ten times!" Avramik answered, his face twisting into something like a smile.

"And starches you too, I suppose."

"She'd also iron me if she could," said Avramik, his smile growing broader.

"No doubt she would!" Misha agreed. "But what's this anthill I hear you've brought in here?"

"An anthill?"

"Yes. I'm told there's a constant line of visitors coming and going like ants. You seem to be pretty popular."

Avramik was embarrassed. "Oh, that. They just want to see how I am. I'll bet they have nothing better to do."

"That's all? Well, that's one way of looking at it. By the way, Mira sends you her regards. She went to the playground with Arnon and will drop by later, when I'm gone."

"When you're gone? Where are you going?"

Misha smiled. His eyes lit up with the gleam that Avramik knew and loved. "It won't be for long. Just a couple of hours."

"Will you be driving via Tsemach?"

"Is there any other way?" Seeing Avramik's worried look, he asked, "Why, what's wrong?"

"Isn't it . . . dangerous? I've heard that our cars have been stoned and shot at."

Tsemach was an Arab village located at the main junction of the Jordan Valley. The road going south continued toward Bet She'an, while the roads running east and north led to the settlements along the Sea of Galilee. There was no other route, no way to avoid the shower of rocks that lay in wait for passing Jewish cars.

Misha slapped Avramik on the leg. "Didn't you notice what we drove back from the hospital in?"

"No. I was in a fog."

"Well then, permit me to inform you that you had the honor of riding in an armored vehicle."

Avramik opened his eyes as wide as his swollen face permitted. "An armored vehicle? What's that?"

"We steel-plated a few of our cars. Two layers of steel with one of wood sandwiched between. It makes them bulletproof."

"And the British let you?"

Misha winked. "We had to grease the right palm."

Avramik sat up in bed. "Grease? I don't get it."

"The English major in the police station at Tsemach doesn't allow armored cars. He doesn't like Jews, either. But he does like money. We gave him a gold watch and he agreed to look the other way. I hope that the station will soon be ours, so the palm-crossing can stop."

"Ours? How?"

"The same way that Tiberias is. What, didn't I tell you?"

Avramik was flabbergasted. While here in the infirmary everything seemed so peaceful, the world outside was turning upside down!

"It's a date to remember," said Misha joyfully. "As of yesterday, the eighteenth of April, 1948, Tiberias is again a Jewish city!"

Avramik clutched at Misha's shirtsleeve. His face was pale. "Does that mean we're at war, Misha? Real war?"

Misha placed his big warm hand over Avramik's small one. "Don't you worry, son. It's not a war we wanted, but since it's started, we'll fight. This isn't Europe," he added, seeing Avramik wince. "We have weapons."

There was a light knock on the door.

"Come in," Misha called, sitting up. Rina opened the door.

"May I come in? I'm not bothering you?"

"Of course not, Rina. It's a perfect time for the changing of the guard," Misha said, slapping Avramik on the shoulder. "Here, take this chair. I'm passing

Avramik on to you like a baton in a relay race."

"You mean you're leaving?" asked Rina uncomfortably.

"Look here, if I don't leave now I might begin to grow roots here. Besides, I'll let you in on a secret: our patient's just pretending. He should really be back in the children's house. It's just that he wants everyone to have a chance to pay a sick call. This is yours."

Misha was gone before Rina could think of an answer, leaving her in the middle of the room with no idea what to do with her hands or eyes. Why had he left her with Avramik, all by herself?

21

Rina felt awkward. It was her first time alone with Avramik since his return from the hospital. She had dared enter only because she knew that Misha was with him, and now Misha had gone and left her. Why had he failed to see how embarrassed she would be?

She glanced quickly at Avramik, then looked back down at the floor. Avramik seemed to sink deeper into his pillow, as though looking for a place to hide. What should she say to him? What could they talk about? Why had she let herself be trapped?

"How are you?" she asked all at once, as if someone else was speaking from her throat.

"Fine," Avramik answered curtly.

"Is it true you're coming back to the children's house soon?"

"So Elka says."

"Do you want to?"

Avramik said nothing. Neither did Rina. Something had been bothering her ever since the day of that wild chase. At last she looked Avramik in the eye and asked, "What made you run to the reservoir? Were you planning to . . . to jump in?"

Avramik threw her a quizzical look. Then he understood.

"What? You thought I wanted to drown myself? Are you crazy? Do you think I have nothing better to do? Believe me, I don't intend to give anyone that satisfaction. No one!"

His voice was strained and tense. What "satisfaction" was he talking about? Who was "no one"?

"I just wanted to be alone," Avramik went on. "By myself. And that was the one place I knew that I would be, that's all."

His face, Rina saw, was burning.

"And so you ran away from me, too? Are you mad at me for running after you?"

"I wanted to be alone," he repeated, although it wasn't exactly an answer. "I wanted to be alone. Don't you get it?"

Agitated, he sat up in bed, his eyes like the windows of a dark room. The words came rapidly now, unchecked, like beads from a necklace that has suddenly broken, scattering all over.

111

"What do you kids know anyway? You're always together, together, together! You get up together, you eat together, you play together, you go to bed together. There's nowhere you can hide or be by yourself! It's a good thing the bathroom door has a lock on it. At least there's that . . ."

Rina wanted to run away. What on earth did he want from her? What had she done to him? But Avramik wouldn't stop.

"Everyone's always sticking his nose into everyone else's business. You can't even close your own clothes closet or your desk drawer. Everyone has to see everything. Everyone can go through your things as much as he likes, and when he's done he'll go tell the teacher on you. 'Alona, Ofra got a new eraser from her aunt in Tel Aviv. It isn't fair.' 'Alona, how come Giyora has a leather belt? If he does, we all should.' 'Rika, look what a mess Avramik's clothes are in. It spoils the way the room looks.' Now maybe you know why I need a box with a lock under my bed."

Avramik's voice seethed with uncontrollable anger.

"I need a place that's my own, that's private, that's just mine! That no idiot from our class can poke around in and tell everyone what he found there. Do you understand?"

Rina didn't answer. Though she would gladly have disappeared from the room had there been a way, she felt riveted to her seat by what Avramik was saying.

"And just in case you think there's a hidden treasure in that box, you might as well know that it's empty. There's nothing in it but darkness."

Rina looked at him unbelievingly.

"You think I'm lying, don't you? Then here, take the key and see for yourself. There's nothing in it but darkness! You still don't believe me? Look, it's true that I used to hide things there. When I was still new. All sorts of stuff. But there's nothing there now. Here, take the key and see what a good laugh I've had! There's nothing but darkness there, nothing at all."

Avramik reached into his pajamas and took out a key that hung from a string on his neck. Rina saw the Star of David glint on its gold chain. She took a deep breath. "Forget it," she said. "No one wants to poke around in your box. And no one wants to take your Star of David either, in case you're interested. Not even Rami. He just loses his temper sometimes and says things he doesn't mean."

Avramik didn't answer. Rina swallowed and went on. "Come to think of it, why don't you put the chain in the box? You know that no one wears such things around here, don't you?"

"Listen," said Avramik with an angry look, "I don't give a damn what anyone does on your kibbutz. I'm not taking this chain off, ever, and that's that!"

"Was it a present from someone?" Rina got up the courage to ask.

"Yes." He looked straight at her. "And if I ever find the man who gave it to me, I'll know what happened to my mother."

There was an awkward silence in the room. Rina stared at the floor. Avramik had never mentioned his mother to her before. Never. What had come over him?

Then, all of a sudden, she realized that something had changed. He had trusted her with his secret. Glancing up at him, she asked, "But how can you find him? Does he live in Palestine?"

"Yes. He was in the Jewish Brigade."

"Do you know his name?"

"No. But look." Avramik showed her the Star of David. "You see the three *Y*'s scratched here? I remember his telling me that his first and last initials were *Y* and that he came from a place that started with a *Y*, too."

"But what makes you think he knows what happened to your mother?"

"Because he took her to the hospital. He promised me he'd visit her there. He promised!"

"Why did she have to go to the hospital?" Rina was sorry the minute she asked, but it was too late.

Avramik leaned against the wall, drew up his knees, and clutched his blanket tightly to his chest. "She had this cough," he said in a choked voice. "She coughed all the time. Every day the farmer who hid us covered the cellar door with big sacks so no one would hear her, and every night he moved them so we could come out to breathe and eat. We hid there a long time. I . . . I don't remember where we were before that. My mother and I kept moving from place to place. I just remember that cellar. It was under a silo. It was always cold and dark there. And I was always hungry. There was nothing but hay to eat all day long. I'd actually chew it, just to have something in my mouth. At night the farmer brought us food. My mother kissed his boots.

He didn't allow her to kiss his hands because he was afraid of catching her cough."

Avramik stared off into space. He was in another place and time, in a remote village in Europe toward the end of World War II, down in a dark, wet cellar.

He went on. "I know what happened to my father. My mother told me. She saw it herself. I know that my father is dead. I was just a small boy then. I don't even remember him. But I didn't see what happened to my mother. Maybe that soldier did. I'd hold her tight to make her stop coughing, because I was afraid the farmer would make us leave if she didn't. No matter how good a person you were, you couldn't risk hiding someone like that. Then one day the farmer came and rolled the sacks away in broad daylight and told us not to be afraid, because the war was over and our own soldiers had arrived. The light was so bright that I shut my eyes and hung on to my mother. She just sat there shaking on the mat. That's all she could do. I really don't know how they got us out of there. I felt something hot — maybe it was the sun — and there were voices drumming in my ear."

"And was that when they took her to the hospital?" Rina asked.

"Yes. The soldier from Palestine took her and brought me to a refugee camp. He promised to bring her back to me when she was better. I wanted to go with her, but she said I shouldn't, that I should trust the soldier from Palestine. So they took me to the camp."

"And that's where Misha found you?"

"Yes. He's my mother's brother. He went to check at the hospital and came back and said that I'd never see her again. But I don't believe it!" Avramik cried out. "Until that soldier with the three Y's comes and tells me what really happened to my mother, I won't believe anyone. Because he's the only one who saw. And he promised to tell me."

"Then why don't you look for him?" asked Rina almost inaudibly.

"I . . . I don't know."

"Maybe," she whispered, "it's because you don't want to find him. Because you're afraid of what he'll tell you."

Avramik winced, like someone exposed to a strong light after hiding too long in the dark. He stared at Rina with burning eyes. "How did you know?"

"I knew because I don't believe it, either."

"You don't believe what?"

"That my father was really killed in the war, in Italy."

"But everyone says he was. They even had a memorial service for him, and everyone came."

"So what?" she challenged. "Everyone says that your mother is dead, too. How can you not believe what Misha told you? He's your own uncle."

"But he didn't see my mother die."

"No one from the kibbutz saw my father get killed, either."

"And you're waiting for him to come back?"

"Yes. All the time."

116

Avramik sat bolt upright. "What do you think happened to him?"

"I think he was just wounded. That there was a mistake. That someone else was killed, not my father."

"Then where is he now?"

"In Italy. In a little village with trees and cows and flowers."

"But why doesn't he come back? The war's been over for more than two years. Why doesn't he come back?"

Like a tidal wave, all her daydreams and night dreams suddenly burst the dam of Rina's silence. She had kept them to herself for so long. She hadn't even told her mother about them. Now they came pouring out of her all at once.

"Because he had a head wound. He doesn't remember anything. He doesn't remember our kibbutz or this country, and he doesn't know where to go. That's why he's waiting there. But I'll find him, and when he sees me, he'll know who I am. I'm sure he will, and then he'll remember everything. He'll be so happy that he'll pick me up and hug me and laugh and dance with me the way he used to do when I was little. And then I'll bring him back to the kibbutz and I'll never let him go away again!"

Rina stopped. The wave had passed. She heard it for another moment, receding, and then there was silence.

As though listening to it too, Avramik said in a low voice, "We have the same dreams, Rina."

Rina nodded and bowed her head.

"You know something?" Avramik went on. "I think I really want to find that man with the Y's now. If I do, I'll ask him what happened to my mother. And if . . . she's not alive anymore . . . that will mean that your father . . . isn't either."

Rina said nothing.

"But if he tells me she's alive, we'll go look for them both. For your father and my mother. Okay?"

Rina nodded. She couldn't say a word.

Avramik sank back into the big soft pillow. He felt weak and tired. Yet he also felt more at peace than he had ever felt before. He shut his eyes.

How long did he lie there resting? An hour? Two? He grew aware of something on his chest. A warm soft tongue licked his face. He opened his eyes. A puppy was curled up on the blanket, a brown, round little dog. Rami was standing by the bed, smiling nervously. Rina wasn't there.

"This is our pup," said Rami. "That is, he's the whole class's, but he's yours most of all. He's yours more than anyone's, Avramik."

22

Rika was having a hard time. It wasn't because of the war. Why should a little thing like a war faze Rika? The only extra work it involved was having a bundle of clothing ready for each boy and girl in case they had to flee to the shelter, seeing to it that the daily schedule was kept despite the flood of rumors reaching them about battles everywhere, and making sure every child went straight to his or her parents after rest hour and didn't wander off somewhere. Really, it wasn't so terrible, especially if you kept in mind that Israel's War of Independence had still not reached the Jordan Valley. By trying hard enough, you could forget all about it, could forget that your turn would come, too . . .

No, it wasn't the war. It was Roughie, the fourth grade's new boxer pup. Roughie was everywhere, Roughie made puddles and messes everywhere, and Roughie did everything he could to make a shambles of the daily routine that Rika had worked so hard to maintain during her four years of housemothering the class.

During rest hour, any hope of anyone's lying quietly disappeared the minute Roughie entered the room.

He tottered pudgily from one child to the next with such a pleading look and touching whimper that one needed a heart of stone to resist picking him up and taking him into bed. Which is where all the trouble began.

"It's my turn now," Ehud announced.

"No it isn't. My quarter of an hour isn't up yet," objected Ofra, in whose lap Roughie was just cuddling up for his afternoon nap.

"But you fed him this morning," Ehud insisted.

"So what?" Ofra argued. "Feeding him isn't as much fun as this is."

Their conversation was interrupted by a yell from Ofra. "Ick!" she screamed, leaping out of bed. "He peed on my sheet!"

Ehud thought that was funny. "It serves you right."

"It really does, Ofra," echoed the other children. "Why didn't you put him outside before he did it?"

"Why are you putting him on the floor now? He's already peed, hasn't he?"

"I've got it," Giyora said happily. "We'll build Ofra a kennel outside and give Roughie her bed, okay?"

Alerted by the laughter, Rika appeared on the scene. "What's going on here, for goodness' sake? Don't tell me it's Roughie again!"

The pungent smell of urine filled the room. Ofra stood by her bed with tears in her eyes. Rika didn't have to be told another thing. After all, it wasn't the first time.

"You took him into bed with you again? What's the

matter with you? If I've told you once, I've told you a thousand times not to do it."

"But he's only a puppy," Rami grumbled. "He was just taken away from his mother. He needs someone big and strong to sleep next to."

One day, when this had happened for the umpteenth time, Rika announced officially, "That does it! From now on, he stays outside. If he was old enough to be taken from his mother, he's not such a little puppy anymore. And besides, if you get him used to sleeping in your beds, you'll never be able to make him stop."

"But we don't want to," said Rami. "Honestly, Rika, we like having him in bed with us."

"Oh, you do? Until he pees, eh? Then suddenly everyone is glad that it wasn't in their bed, that the victim was someone else. How would you like it to be you, Rami?"

Rami looked to the other children for support. He didn't know what to say. No one looked back.

"And what about his droppings in the corners?" asked Rika, still on the offensive. "I don't see anyone hurrying to clean them up, either."

Shai and Brochi, who were nearest the doorway, began to make a careful break for it. When Rika went on the warpath, it was best to steer clear of her.

"Oh no you don't!" she cried, nabbing them in time. "No one's leaving now, is that clear? If rest hour has been ruined anyway, we might as well put it to good use. I want to know once and for all, whose puppy is this?"

"It's all of ours!" the children shouted. "It belongs to the whole class."

Rika placed her hands belligerently on her hips, which made her look like a two-handled kettle about to boil. And she was boiling, too.

"And you all think that this is how to bring up a dog? With so many parents he'll turn out to be a juvenile delinquent. He needs one child to be responsible for him, to housebreak him, to take him out for walks, and to feed him on schedule."

"But we feed him all the time," said Keren bravely.

"And you think that's good for him?" asked Rika, pointing at Roughie. He was curled up between a sheet and a pillowcase in his private little paradise, eyeing the argument drowsily. "Just look at him. Do you think it's good for a dog to be so fat? In the end you'll wind up with a big, fat, lazy monster who'll take over your beds and drive you all out of here."

"But Rika, what are you talking about?" asked Giyora. "In the first place, he's not fat. All puppies are a little chubby. They get over it —"

A gale of laughter interrupted him. Not even Rika could keep a straight face. Giyora looked down at his own tubby frame and broke into a broad, moony grin.

"What are you laughing at?" he asked innocently. "Can't you see I'm still a puppy myself?"

The tension that had been building in the room vanished in another wave of laughter. But though it was gone, Rika would not relent. "All right," she said quietly. "You can feed him until he bursts. But outside. From now on he eats and sleeps outside. And if I catch any of you taking him to bed, I'll have Misha take him right back to Yavne'el!"

Avramik stepped up to the puppy and stroked its soft fur.

"Rika," he said, "I'll train him. Honest. I'll take him out when he needs to go and teach him not to go to the bathroom inside, okay? And I'll give him the box beneath my bed. I'll line it with something soft so he can sleep in it. Just let him stay with us, all right? Don't make him live alone outside. He needs company. He doesn't want to be alone."

Rika looked from Avramik to the puppy and back again.

"He's *afraid* to be left alone," said Avramik, carefully lifting the puppy. Roughie did not object. He curled up in Avramik's arms as though he felt right at home there.

"All right," said Rika gently. "If you're willing to be responsible, go ahead. Are you sure you won't miss your box, though?"

"I'm sure," answered Avramik.

"Positively?" asked Rika skeptically.

"Positively!" declared Avramik with a glance of complicity at Rina. A shiver ran down her back, followed by a warm wave. Better a puppy in the box than just darkness, no?

23

So the puppy stayed in the children's house, living happily in the box under Avramik's bed.

The name "Roughie" was Avramik's gift to the puppy, too. That is a story in itself.

When Avramik was still in the infirmary and woke to find the puppy curled up on his blanket, he did not have much time to regard the warm cuddly thing that was already licking his face. Rami, too, who was standing there with a nervous grin, had no time to say what he had planned to because, bony and dressed in white, Elka was looming in the doorway like an avenging angel.

"What's that?" she asked in an ominous voice.

"It's . . . it's . . ." Rami stammered. "It's a dog. It's a boxer pup. It's Maya's grandson."

"Maya's grandson, eh? Well, I don't care if it's the grandson of Alexander the Great. If it's a dog, it stays out of here. Is that clear?"

"Yes," said Rami, barely stifling the laugh that was tickling his throat. Avramik stole a glance at him and swallowed a smile. They batted the joke back and forth like a Ping-Pong ball. The idea: a puppy dog in Elka's spick-and-span infirmary!

But Elka's dander was up. "And if you're well enough to take care of the famous Maya's grandson, Avramik, I suggest you pack your bags and kindly return to the children's house. I'd like to see the welcome Rika gives you!"

The puppy seemed to disapprove of Elka's tone, because he jumped up and down on his stubby legs and yipped in a high, babyish voice. "Yip, yip!" And he scurried under the blanket. Safety first!

The two boys giggled, Rami's laughter bubbling out like champagne from an uncorked bottle. The guilty feeling he'd been carrying around with him ever since Avramik ran away was suddenly gone. There was no longer any need to explain or apologize.

Before long the three of them were the center of attention in the children's house.

"Wow!" said Naomi when she saw them appear in the doorway. "What a cute puppy. Didn't I tell you Rami's father would surprise us?"

"He's a beauty!" said Giyora. "But what happened to his tail?"

Ehud gave Giyora an incredulous look. "You mean you don't know? He's a boxer."

"So what if he's a boxer?"

"Boxer pups' tails are cut off as soon as they're born."

"But why?" Naomi was close to tears. "Why be so mean to the poor things?"

"It's for their own good, silly," said Ehud. "If they get hurt in the tail, it can damage their spine."

"Honestly?" asked Naomi, her tears drying up instantly.

"I swear. Ask Rami. Rami, isn't that what your dad told us?"

"It sure is."

"What a funny face he has," said Keren. "Like an old man's."

"What old man are you talking about?" Rami growled. "He's a boxer, not a bulldog. It's the bulldogs that have the funny, wrinkled faces and short legs, not the boxers."

"He's awfully sweet," declared Naomi, stroking the puppy's brown back as he huddled fearfully in Rami's arms. "What should we call him?"

"Lightning," said Shai. "That's a real nice name."

"But what if he's slow as molasses?" Ehud asked doubtfully.

"Then Hero. Or Champion."

"But what if he's a scaredy-cat?"

"That's enough out of you, Ehud," Rami ordered, forgetting that he was no longer king of the class and that no one listened to him anymore. "This puppy isn't going to be any coward. He's Maya's grandson. Even Elka didn't fool around with him."

Avramik looked at Rami and they both began to laugh. Only now did the children notice that Avramik was unexpectedly back from the infirmary — and with Rami! And that something had happened between them because they were laughing together. The awkward capsule the children had been in for the last several days burst open, and in their relief they began to laugh, too, and to call out all sorts of names.

126

"Let's call him Mutsi-Putsi!"

"No, Ishkabibble!"

"Nebuchadnezzar!"

"No! Piccolino!"

"Fidolino!"

"I've got it," said Avramik, whom no one heard because of the general commotion.

"Quiet!" called Rami. "Avramik has an idea. Let him talk."

The uproar died down. Rami might be a deposed king, but as Avramik's herald he still counted for something. In fact, for a great deal.

"We're looking for a name for the dog, right?" Avramik said. "Well, why don't we ask him what he wants to be called?"

"But how can we ask him?" Giyora demanded.

Avramik didn't bother to answer. There was something changed about him, a new confidence, as though he had finally taken root. He turned to the boxer pup. "What would you like to be called?" he asked, taking the dog from Rami's arms.

"Ruff, ruff!" yipped the pup.

"There!" said Avramik. "You see? We'll call him Roughie. It's a perfect name for a boxer."

"Roughie?" asked Naomi, savoring it on her tongue. "That's just as weird as the other names."

"No it isn't," Rami declared. "Roughie's a nice name, and it's kind of special, too."

"For God's sake," said Ofra, "I've never heard of a dog called Roughie before."

"Well, you're hearing of one now," Rami told her. And turning to the puppy he said, "Roughie's a terrific name, isn't it, Roughie?"

The tubby pup looked at him in a bratty way and barked, "Ruff! Ruff!" with satisfaction. That settled it. Roughie had chosen his own name. What more could anyone say?

24

Roughie's meals were no simple matter.

Who didn't want to feed him? Everyone did: Rami, Naomi, Ehud, Ofra, Shai, Brochi. In short, the entire fourth grade. Yet first among equals, of course, was Avramik, who was responsible for all Roughie's needs, including the less pleasant ones. It was Avramik who cleaned up after him if he did something naughty in the corner and Avramik who — if only he had had some — would have sprayed the room with French perfume to stay on Rika's good side. And since every cloud has its silver lining, it was Avramik whose job it was to feed Roughie, which he did once a day after lunch. The only problem was that because the puppy naturally favored whoever fed him, and because the slurpy, chewy, gurgly way he ate was such fun to listen to, and most of all, because when he was done he rolled over on his back to let his tubby tummy get petted, the children fed him constantly. His life became one endless meal interrupted only by school hours, which was a lucky thing for his digestion.

It drove Rika up the wall. "Naomi, why don't you finish your cocoa? Who are you saving it for?"

"For Roughie."

"But Roughie doesn't drink cocoa!"

"Maybe he'd like to try some. Anyway, I'm not thirsty."

A petulant whine came from the front porch. Rami moved his chair back and stood up.

"Rami!" Rika exclaimed. "Where are you going?"

"Who, me? I finished eating. I'm full."

"And everything you've left on your plate goes to Roughie, eh? Your father's told you a thousand times that a boxer pup should be fed only once a day if you don't want to make him sick."

Rami grinned sheepishly. He'd been caught in the act again. Life wasn't easy with a housemother who saw everything. How could one possibly be expected to obey such an order?

At lunchtime, seeing Brochi neglect his hamburger, Alona joined the fray. "I don't understand you," she said, her eyes scolding the children as only a teacher's can do. "Do you have any idea where you're living? Do you know what's happening in this country right now? There's fighting everywhere. Jerusalem is under siege; people are going hungry and thirsty there. Why, not even the children in Jerusalem have enough to eat. And here you are throwing food away, giving it to a puppy who can barely bring himself to sniff at it because he's so stuffed already. If only you knew what the situation is and that it's likely to be the same here in the Valley, too."

"In a minute she'll be telling us about the starving children in India," thought Giyora. "I know it all by heart." One look from Alona, however, was enough to make him keep his thoughts to himself.

"You'd better get this straight," she told them. "From now on everyone's eating what's on his plate! If there's anything left for the puppy when you're through, fine. If there isn't, you can take turns going to the main kitchen for scraps."

"But they won't give us scraps there," said Rami. "I've already tried."

"Who won't?"

"Fat Sarah, the kitchen head."

"Why won't she?"

"She says that human food isn't for dogs. That it musn't be wasted. That even the scraps should be eaten."

"That's why she's so fat." Brochi laughed. "She probably eats them all herself. She's ten times worse than Giyora."

Alona silenced him with a look. It was nothing to joke about.

Sarah, the kitchen head, had arrived in the kibbutz right after World War II. Her cheeks had been sunken and her clothes had hung loosely, as though on a hanger. She wouldn't look at anyone and hardly talked to anyone. Her husband and her little baby, it was said, had disappeared "over there." The kibbutz children kept away from her because she scared them. Once she moved in with Shmulik the barn hand, however, she began to show signs of change. She no longer stared at the ground when she spoke, and sometimes she gossiped with the other women at work. When she first started putting on weight — she was working in the kitchen by then and eating all the time — it was attributed to her pregnancy. "It's normal," said her friends. "She'll thin down again when she gives birth." But Sarah gave birth and grew no thinner. On the contrary. She went right on eating huge portions at meals and generous snacks between them, until she became so enormous that Leahleh, the chief gossip in the laundry, began to tell everyone, "Sarah's gotten to be as wide as she is tall."

"It's because she's still nursing," said those who gave her the benefit of the doubt. "She needs the calories."

"No it isn't," said those who did not. "She'll never stop eating. She'll be fat for the rest of her life."

And, indeed, Sarah retained her voracious appetite after she stopped nursing.

Rami didn't make his second scraps expedition for Roughie by himself. He took Avramik with him — and the puppy, too, of course. Yet by the time he entered the kitchen with an empty bowl in his hand he found himself alone with three women who sat peeling potatoes around a huge pot of water. The three were talking about Kibbutz Gesher, the southernmost settlement in the Jordan Valley, which had repelled a determined Arab attack the day before.

"Did you hear that they evacuated all the children?" asked Rochi, who was holding a potato from which hung a long ribbon of peel. "They had to carry the babies and the kindergarten children in their arms." The plop of the potato in cold water punctuated the sentence.

Estherke, who sat squarely over a crate that was filling up with potato peels at a terrific rate, gave out marks as usual. "You've got to hand it to those kibbutz-niks from Ashdot Ya'akov. I heard they met the men from Gesher halfway and helped them carry the children across the ravine, and that then they brought them back with them and put them up in their own children's house. They gave them beds, too, or at least mattresses."

A potato chucked into the pot by Estherke sprayed water over Rami, who had been standing behind her and listening.

"Hey!" he cried. "Watch it! What's the matter with you?"

"Rami, watch your big tongue," said Estherke. "That's no way to talk to a grown-up. And what are you doing here anyway? You look like Oliver Twist come to beg for a bowl of soup."

"I'd like a little meat for our puppy, Roughie. Just the scraps. Do you have anything left over from yesterday?"

"Go ask Sarah. She's in charge of the kitchen," said

Rochi, nodding toward the outsize figure who was occupied with the shelves of the refrigerator. "It's up to her."

Rami glanced back at the door. Darn! Where were Avramik and Roughie? A fine time they had picked to disappear, leaving him to fight their battles. Seeing that he had no choice, though, he bravely cleared his throat. "Sarah," he said hesitantly. "Sarah, maybe —"

The door of the large refrigerator slammed shut. Sarah wheeled around and looked down at Rami from her majestic height. "I heard you," she said brusquely. "There's no dog food here!"

"But dogs have to eat, too. They have a right to live also, don't they?"

Sarah's hands rested on her hips like the handles of a full storage jar. Yet though her body, heavy with authority, was in the kibbutz kitchen, her eyes were far away. Her arms dropped limply to her sides.

"Dogs aren't for Jews," she said in a changed voice. "Dogs are for Christians. Dogs bite Jews. The food in this kitchen is for Jews."

Rami backed away from her. He was more frightened by the way she spoke now than by the way she had scolded him at first. The words seemed to come from somewhere else, from a dark, distant world that he didn't belong to, that he didn't want to belong to.

He glanced at the three women peeling potatoes, looking for reassurance. No one said a word. Their eyes were cast down, focused on the movements of their starch-covered hands, which were even busier than usual. "It's hopeless," he told himself, starting to retreat toward the door "I'll have to look someplace else." Turning to go, he saw Avramik's slender outline in the doorway. The sunlight streamed down Avramik's back, but his expressionless face was in shadow. For a minute he stood there without moving. Then, leaving the sunlit doorway, he stepped up to Sarah. The dark outline turned into a boy. In his face, clearly visible now, was a look that Rami had never seen there before. Was it tension, determination, or something else that he would never be able to understand?

Sarah stared down at Avramik. Her look was still remote, from "over there." Avramik stared back at her. Trustingly, unconcernedly, the puppy cuddled in his arms.

Rami couldn't say how long they stood there like that. The silence grew so unbearable that he wanted to scream, to run wherever his legs would carry him. And then Sarah blinked, ran a dreamy hand over her forehead, and reached out to take the bowl from Rami.

From then on the puppy had all the food he could eat.

And from then on, too, Rami kept asking himself three questions. Why had Avramik first hidden behind the door instead of entering the kitchen? What had made him come in? And what had made Sarah change her mind and fill the bowl with good things?

He thought about it for a couple of weeks, until something happened that changed everything. Events took on a momentum of their own, and new problems made the old ones seem unimportant, questions that could be postponed until peace came again.

25

That Friday afternoon Rami burst into his parents' room, perspiring and out of breath.

"Mom, where's the cold water? I'm dying of thirst."

Misha, who was bent over the radio, impatiently signaled him to be quiet.

"But where's the water?" Rami asked in a loud voice. He looked around him. "I can't find the jar."

Misha turned up the volume. The five o'clock news blared from the big brown box that confidently took up a whole corner of the room, as though it knew it was indispensable.

"Cripes!" Rami grumbled. "The news again! You can't do anything when it's on. I could drop dead from thirst and no one would even notice."

Mira rose quickly from the old armchair and took him out to the porch. "The water jar is here," she said, drawing the curtain of the cupboard. "The hot weather's about to begin, so I put it in its usual summer place."

Rami grabbed the earthenware jar, put his lips to its mouth, and tilted his head back, his throat going in and out as he swallowed.

"Hey! Leave some for me!" Avramik yelled, running

up from the main lawn with Roughie at his heels. The fat pup bounded after him on his stubby legs, catching up, tumbling, and catching up again. Life was one big game for him. When they reached the porch Roughie sat on his hind legs and looked worshipfully up at Avramik, his panting tongue hanging out as if to say "That was great, but what do you have planned for me next?"

Avramik took the enamel bowl and filled it from the faucet in the garden. "Here, drink. You must be thirsty."

As the puppy loudly guzzled the water, Avramik turned to his cousin. "What are you, a camel?" he asked. "How much can you drink? Leave some for me!"

Rami finally tore the jar away from his mouth. "Here," he said. "I left you some."

The news came to an end and they heard the familiar click of the radio being switched off. In the sudden silence the room seemed to echo like a seashell in which you can hear the boom of the sea. Avramik drained the last drops from the jar and anxiously put it down. There was a look on Misha's face that he had never seen before: half light and half shadow, half joy and half sorrow, half relief and half worry. Avramik didn't know what to make of it.

"What happened?" he asked, standing the jar on the floor while keeping his eyes on Misha. He was still as sensitive and anxious about Misha's moods as though he were a puppy himself.

Misha hesitated, groping for the right words. Finally,

he straightened up and said solemnly, "We have a state, a Jewish state. The State of Israel was officially declared today!"

"But what else, Misha? Something else happened, too."

"Yes it did," said Misha, downcast. "A whole group of villages near Jerusalem has surrendered to the Arab Legion. The radio didn't say how many dead and wounded there were, but the survivors were all taken prisoner."

Mira went back out to the porch, a frown on her usually beaming face. "I never thought it would be like this. Here we've been waiting for a Jewish state for so long, and when it's finally declared, it has to be on such a tragic day."

"And this is only the beginning," said Misha softly, as though to himself. "Who knows what may happen tomorrow . . . even tonight . . ."

He stood there motionless for a moment, still thinking about the news. Then he looked up and laid his hands on the boys' shoulders.

"What's new with you kids?" he asked. "Have you been having shelter drills?"

"You bet," Rami answered, glad to be asked. Now he had something to tell his father about. "You should have seen the last one. We ran like wild Indians, doubled over — here, like this. We ran all the way from the children's house in the trench, and I'll bet that if there'd been Arabs right above us they wouldn't even have known we were there."

Mira turned pale and looked anxiously at Misha.

"Don't worry," said Misha. "They won't be here so soon. And at the first sign of danger, we'll make sure to evacuate the children."

"It's fun running down trenches," said Rami. "But if they won't be here so soon, what are we scared of?"

"Of bombs and artillery," said Avramik.

"What do you know about bombs and artillery?" asked Rami, and then he felt so sorry that he almost bit his tongue. "What a dope I am," he thought, "to ask someone from "over there," who went through the war, what he knows about bombs and artillery. It's like . . . like . . ." He stood there sheepishly, unable to finish the thought. At last, though, shaking off unpleasant thoughts, he said loudly, "You want to play tag with the kids on the main lawn? Let's go."

"Just a minute, Rami," said Mira. "Are your clothes all ready?"

"Which clothes, the ones for the shelter?"

"Yes."

"Sure they are. Haven't you seen that each of us has a bundle beneath his bed?"

"No, I didn't notice," Mira confessed. "I've been too busy making bundles for the third grade."

She stood there wanting to hug them both, or at least to put an arm around them. But Rami was no longer tied to her apron strings. He didn't like her to be "mushy," as he called it. As for Avramik, he had kept his distance from her since the day he came to the kibbutz. Thank God she still had little Arnon to cuddle. She looked at the two boys and Roughie. "Three puppy dogs," she thought. "That's all they are, the three of them."

Just then Roughie bristled. Huddling close to Avramik, he let out a low growl that could have been either a challenge or an alarm. There was something strange in the air. The trill of evening bird songs continued as before, and the spring flowers gave off the same scent, but something menacing hung above the peace and quiet, hovering over the cries of playing children and the distant lowing of the cows in the barn. Something was about to happen.

26

War came all at once to the villages of the Jordan Valley. Three armies — the Jordanian, the Iraqi, and the Syrian — advanced on it simultaneously. Early that Saturday morning, the day after Israel's Declaration of Independence, tanks followed by soldiers began pouring down from the mountains across the river.

At the crack of dawn the door of the children's house swung open. Rika and Alona appeared in the doorway.

"Good morning," said Rika, more loudly than usual. "Everyone up!"

Avramik, who was lying in bed with Roughie curled on top of him, knew right away what that meant. Rika's voice was like the lull before a storm, like a bell that makes itself ring clearly and coolly when what it really wants to toll is Danger! Danger!

All night Avramik had sensed the danger coming. Since yesterday Roughie had been growling and whimpering because of that something in the air. As though for protection, he had slept in Avramik's arms. Now, seeing Rika and Alona, Avramik felt better. At last the mysterious threat had a form.

"I want everyone up and dressed," said Rika in a tight voice. "And everyone take the bundles beneath your beds. We're going to the shelter."

"But Rika, it's Saturday." Naomi protested sleepily from the next room. "We can sleep all we want."

"What are you doing here, Rika?" Rami asked. "On Saturdays the parents are on duty."

Alona went from room to room. "Naomi! Rami! Wake up! We're going to the shelter. Get dressed quickly and take your bundles, do you hear me?"

"Yes," said Naomi, rousing herself and getting out of bed. "I'll bet it's just another drill to see how fast we can get there," she added, searching for the sleeves of her shirt.

"They wouldn't drill us on a Saturday," said Rina. "This time it's for real!"

Her heart pounded. The quiet around them was un-natural, unreal. Avramik was standing next to her, his bundle of clothes in one hand and Roughie in the other. Suddenly she wanted Avramik to touch her, just for a second. Since making their secret pact in the infirmary, they had hardly exchanged a word. But something had changed. They were no longer the same children. Although they didn't know what to call it, something had sprung up between them.

Avramik's shoulder rubbed against hers. "Come on," he said. "Let's get at the end of the line."

Why at the end? Rina wanted to ask. But Alona was hushing the excited children and counting them off.

"One, two, three . . . five . . . eight . . . ten. There's one missing. Who is it?"

"It's Naomi," said Giyora. "She always dawdles."

"Fourth grade!" called a voice from outside. "What's taking you so long? Get to the shelter!"

Naomi emerged from her room carrying the one-eared teddy bear that she always slept with.

"I knew she was looking for her teddy." Giyora sneered. "Like a baby! What a dope —"

"Be quiet!" said Alona sharply. "This is no time for fights. Everyone out to the trench, quickly! Enter the shelter as soon as you reach it, so there's no crowding outside. All right, run!"

The network of trenches crisscrossing the kibbutz suddenly came alive. One by one the children's houses emptied and their occupants hurried to the shelters.

Rina jogged quickly at the end of the line, in front of Avramik and Alona, who brought up the rear. A feeling of relief, even an odd happiness, came over her: at last "it" was happening on their kibbutz, too. The daily routine would be broken. There would be no school. What a lark!

The trenches were dug in straight lines from the children's houses to the shelters. They crossed the green lawns and ran through flower gardens and past thick-rooted trees. Rina nearly tripped over one of the roots sticking up from the bottom of the trench.

"Watch where you're going," said Avramik. "You don't want to fall now."

The dark entrance of the shelter stood at the end of the trench, emitting a dense, stuffy smell of tar and varnish. One by one the children vanished into it. Despite Alona's prodding, Rina paused at the top of the steps to look behind her. Avramik wasn't there. He was crouched nearby in the trench, his head bent low over Roughie, whom he hugged as though for dear life.

"Avramik," cried Rina, "come to the shelter!"

Avramik looked up. "I'm staying here! I'm not going into that hole!"

"But why not? Everyone else is inside already."

Avramik sat down with his back to the wall of the trench. He didn't answer. Rina didn't know what to do. She felt he had planned it all long ago and that nothing could make him change his mind.

"In you go, Rina," said Alona. "Leave Avramik to me."

Just then something whistled through the air. A hand reached out of the shelter and pulled Alona inside. The whistle turned into a horrible shriek. Something landed on the roof of one of the children's houses and exploded with a deafening roar.

Roughie leaped from Avramik's arms and ran full tilt into Rina. Together the two of them tumbled down the steps of the shelter. A second whistle emitted its hair-raising warning, and soon a second shell crashed nearby.

The battle of the Jordan Valley had begun.

27

The first artillery barrage landed on the kibbutz just as the last of the infants and younger children were being herded into the shelters. Because there wasn't room for everyone, the "big" children, those from the fifth grade up, took cover in the trenches. There hadn't been time to build enough shelters, and that was the next best place. Avramik stayed with them.

Rina, having gone sprawling with Roughie down the dirt steps of the shelter just as the first shell exploded, landed on Alona's soft frame. For a moment she lay there stunned, the shriek of the shell still resounding in her ears. Alona picked herself up heavily and pulled Rina after her.

"Are you all right?"

Rina nodded. Her whole body ached and she would have burst into tears had she tried to answer. In the dim light trickling into the shelter she saw the puppy trembling at her feet. Next to him was a small puddle. She forgot her own pain immediately.

"Is he hurt?" she asked in fright. "What is that? Blood?"

"Of course not," answered Alona. "He's just so scared that he peed. Take him inside right away, Rina. Staying here by the entrance is dangerous."

Inside the old shelter, which had been built during World War II, a few kerosene lamps dueled with the darkness. Bunk beds, supported by thin wooden posts running from floor to ceiling, lined the walls. A heavy, oppressive odor of freshly sawed and stained wood mingled with the stale-breath smell of the children and filled the narrow space. Three grades were crammed into it, and like beans in a bag, it took much time and maneuvering for everyone to find a place.

"Will the fourth grade please gather near the south entrance," Rika announced. "I want you all to sit down."

Several children had clambered into the upper bunks. There, feeling as though they had arrived in the Promised Land, they sat watching the others milling below. "Hey, Ehud," called Giyora, "can I sit next to you up there? Save me a place."

"Are you kidding? With a fatso like you we'll crash down on the kids below."

"Baloney!" said Giyora, starting up the ladder. "You just don't want to move over."

He sat next to Ehud and let his feet dangle like those of the children next to him, swinging them back and forth as though from a tree branch. Everything was still new and interesting, an adventure.

"Is there any more room up there?" Rina asked.

"Sorry," said Giyora, who a minute ago had been an underdog himself. "We're all sold out."

"Who says?" said Alona. "You'll have to shove over. I want three children sitting in every bunk."

"But there's no room," Giyora argued.

"Then one of you will have to sit behind a post with his feet on either side."

"But that's not comfortable."

"No, it isn't, but you have no choice. You can take turns."

"But I'm big enough for two," Giyora said. "You can't possibly get one more up here."

Ehud laughed. "A minute ago you were telling me how thin you were. Now it suits you to be fat again, huh?"

"I'm coming up," Rina announced, bending over to pick up Roughie. Alona stopped her.

"Don't even think of it, Rina. Do you want him to pee on the heads of the children below you? You've seen what happens to him when he's frightened."

"It can happen to one of us, too," Rina grumbled. "And besides, how long do you expect us to stay here?"

"You'll stay here as long as you have to," said Rika impatiently. "Will you please sit down, Rina? I have to count you all."

Rina resignedly found a place on a lower bunk. She wrapped Roughie in a towel and held him curled up anxiously in her arms. Gradually, his little body stopped trembling with fear. Had Rami wanted to take the puppy now, Rina would never have agreed. But there was no danger of his asking. Rami was happy in his "penthouse" and had no intention of moving down-stairs.

Rika counted the fourth-graders once again.

"I don't get it," she murmured. "Someone's missing. Mira," she called out to the other end of the shelter, "is one of our children with you?"

"Don't frighten her," said Alona to Rika in a low voice. "It's Avramik. He stayed outside in the trench."

"But why?" Rika protested. "Why isn't he in the shelter?"

"Because he refused to enter it," Alona whispered. "He must be claustrophobic. Did you forget that he spent all of World War Two in a cellar?"

"I'd better check on him," Rika replied, starting quickly up the steps.

By now Mira, who was the third-grade housemother, had finished counting her children, too. "No," she called back to Rika, "none of your children is here. Who's missing?"

There was a dull boom outside.

"That one landed farther off," said Giyora profes-sionally. "Nearer the chicken run."

"How do you know?" Ehud asked. "It's hard to tell from in here."

"Leave it to an expert."

"Giyora, stop swinging your legs. You almost kicked me," said Mira, making her way down the narrow aisle. "Who's missing?" she asked again worriedly, trying to make out Alona's face in the dim light.

Someone came down the stairs. It was Rika, who entered quickly and said, still straining to see in the semidarkness, "You're right, Alona. He said he's had enough of 'holes' like this. He told me that nothing could make him come inside."

Mira let out a muffled cry. "It's Avramik. He's still out there."

Alona grabbed her arm, blocking her path. "Don't go back up now, Mira," she said. "It won't do any good. He's with the fifth-graders. They're not alone. They have a teacher and a housemother, too."

Mira tried to squirm loose.

"If they can be up there, so can he," said Alona. "The trench is plenty deep. Don't worry."

Mira wavered. Speaking as if she was the commander of the shelter, Alona went on firmly, "You have to stay with your class. That's your first responsibility. And believe me, it wouldn't help even if you tried. He's as stubborn as a mule."

Mira hung her arms helplessly. She knew how stubborn Avramik could be. She knew, too, that she had no chance of coaxing him into the shelter. From his first day in the kibbutz he had let her know that she wasn't his mother and couldn't tell her what to do. Still, Avramik was one of her "puppy dogs," and she wanted all of them with her in the shelter. He may not have wanted to be one, yet who knew? Maybe someday . . .

28

Rina woke from a dream-troubled sleep. Her whole body ached from sitting all day and night in the shelter. Something was pressing like a lead weight on her left shoulder. It was the head of Naomi, who had been the first to fall asleep last night and was now propped against her like a fragile plant seeking support.

It was dim in the shelter. The kerosene lamps had nearly gone out, though the one by the entrance was burning a bit more brightly than the others. A sudden draft caused its light to flicker over Rika, who had dozed off on the floor with her back against the wall.

Rina carefully lifted Naomi's head from her sore shoulder. It swung through the air like a pendulum and slowly came to rest on the shoulder of the child sleeping on her other side.

"It's like a magic spell," Rina thought. "How can anyone sleep like that sitting up?"

Someone sighed in her sleep. Someone else muttered a few words and fell silent. The air was stuffy with kerosene, brooding, and the breathing of the children. Slowly Rina slipped off the wooden bunk and stood on the rough concrete floor. Her bare feet rubbed against something soft and warm: Roughie. The puppy awoke

and came to life instantly, as though he had been waiting for this moment. Jumping to his little feet he ran to
the entrance of the shelter as if it was obvious that
Rina had gotten up just so he could have a breath of
fresh air and get a whiff of the big wide world. He was
in such a hurry that he ran right into Rika, whose legs
were stretched across the aisle, and went sprawling.
Though he regained his feet at once and hopped gaily
up the stairs, Rika was awake.

"What is it? Rina? Where are you going?"

"Couldn't I please go outside for a while?" whispered
Rina. "I feel as if I'm choking in here. And anyhow,
Roughie ran away. He must have to go to the bath-
room. I'll bring him back when he's done."

Rika deliberated. The silence weighed heavily.
Above the entrance a lone cricket chirped. The fighting
had temporarily died down.

"All right," she agreed. "But just for a few minutes,
and don't go far. And come back as soon as Roughie's
finished, okay?"

"Okay."

In the shelter, night was eternal, but outside the
dawn was beginning to break. A bluish light filtered
through the pine trees, dropping softly on a fallen pine
cone and a carpet of needles. In a nearby garden,
flowers trembled in the morning breeze. Heavy with
dew, the snapdragons stood proudly erect, their pur-
plish silver shoots giving off a tantalizing, honey-sweet
smell. A rooster in the far-off chicken run crowed
cockily, and was followed by a second and a third.
The cows were mooing in the barn, waiting to be fed

and milked. In a tree close by, a blackbird began to sing, its voice full of mysterious longing. A person might think there were no wars anywhere.

Roughie came bounding out of the bushes, merry and playful as usual. He licked Rina's bare feet and tried biting them.

Rina kicked him gently. "Oof, you're tickling me. Go find another game."

The tubby little pup stopped short, his square boxer face crinkling with wonder as he sniffed the breeze. Suddenly he hopped down into a trench and leaped onto the first of a long line of dark forms, tugging at its gray blanket until it began to stir and kick. A hand groped from beneath the blanket and found the happily quivering dog, while a second hand stroked its back. Like a lost child reunited with his parents, Roughie began to bark and whimper with joy.

"Shhh!" said Avramik, pulling the blanket off his head. "Be quiet, you shrimp, do you hear me? Everyone's sleeping."

The row of gray blankets began to move. A head rose out of the trench and said sleepily, "Can't you get rid of him? Just when the shelling's stopped and there's finally some quiet, you have to wake us all up."

Avramik took Roughie in his arms. "Come on," he said, "let's get out of here."

The puppy whined excitedly, licking the boy's face.

"Shhh! Be quiet, you little rascal."

A clod of earth broke loose and fell into the trench. Avramik, looking up, saw Rina standing on the earthworks above him. In the pale morning light he could make out a broad grin on her face.

"Good morning," he said a little awkwardly. "Did they let you out of the shelter?"

"Yes," said Rina. "I woke up early. Everyone else is still asleep."

"How is it in there?" asked Avramik, climbing out of the trench.

Rina kicked at a pebble, sending it flying off into the flowers, where it stirred up a shower of dewdrops.

"So-so," she said. "I'd rather be out here in the trench."

"But why? It's much more dangerous here. A couple of shells came pretty close. Look at our house."

Rina turned to look and couldn't believe her eyes. The children's house had taken a direct hit. The red tile roof had been blown away in all directions and there was a gaping hole in one of the walls. The long white wall of the nearby nursery was scarred, too.

"I'd still rather be out here," she said. "You can't imagine how crowded it is in there. And how stuffy and boring. Rika and Alona do their best to think up games and sing songs and tell stories, but how long can you go on sitting like sardines without doing anything?"

"But you do go out sometimes. I've seen you take turns between shellings. Alona and Rika have been to visit me."

Roughie barked sharply.

"And so have you, haven't you?" Avramik asked him.

Roughie happily waggled his rear and disappeared into a dark green rosemary bush.

Rina shrugged. "They let us out sometimes for a breath of fresh air, because Alona herself says how hot and hard to breathe it is in there. But it's just for a few minutes, and then it's back into the 'hole' again."

"I've heard it's even worse in the babies' shelter. They say there's a hundred and twenty of them there."

"What, babies?"

"A hundred and twenty? Of course not. Babies, nursing mothers, and the whole nursery and kindergarten. Just think of how hot and crowded and smelly it must be. Can you imagine a whole shelter full of diapers?"

"And dirty ones at that." Rina laughed.

Avramik grew serious. "What are they saying about me in there?"

"Who?"

"The kids in our class."

Rina didn't know what to say.

"That depends," she finally answered. "It depends who —"

"I'll bet Giyora and Ehud say I'm chicken."

"They did at first. They said you were scared of the shelter, but Rami really let them have it. They almost had a fistfight."

Avramik plucked a sprig of rosemary and rolled it between his fingers. The white knuckles of his clenched hand betrayed his emotion.

"Rami sticks up for you all the time now," Rina added. "He says that it's natural for you not to want to be in the shelter, and that it takes courage to stay out in the trench when the shells are falling all around."

Avramik shredded the rosemary leaves, releasing their sharp smell into the air.

"I . . . It is scary out here. Sometimes, when a shell comes close, I'm frightened to death. But I just can't go into the shelter. That's even worse!"

Roughie, who had been poking about in the bushes and was drunk from the scents and fresh air, barked gaily and bounded back onto the pavement. Then they heard footsteps: a pair of weary boots, heavy with responsibility. Roughie charged around a corner, his barks turning into yips of excitement. Who could it be?

29

Misha appeared around the corner.

"Hey, what are you two lovebirds doing out here?"

He drew near with heavy steps. With him was Tsvika, a high school junior whose sandals clicked briskly on the pavement.

"Seriously, what are you doing out here?"

"It's quiet now," said Avramik lamely. "The shellings have stopped."

"They can start again any minute," Misha warned in a hoarse voice. Now that he was standing beside them, Avramik could see how bloodshot and puffy from sleeplessness his eyes were. A two-days' growth of beard showed on his chin and there was a new crease in his brow.

"If they do, we'll jump into the trench," said Avramik. "I'm out here with the fifth-graders anyway."

Misha laid a large hand on the boy's head. "So I've heard," he said.

Tsvika, who had a gun slung over one shoulder, stood off to the side with his hands in his pockets, soldier style. His shirt was unbuttoned and a lock of hair fell nonchalantly over his forehead. Avramik stared at him. "You look like a real soldier," he said, a tinge of envy in his voice.

"That's just what he's trying to look like," said Misha, his face relaxing into a smile. "You couldn't have given him a bigger compliment."

"But what kind of rifle have you got there, Tsvika?" Avramik asked. "Isn't that a shotgun? I'll be darned if it isn't — yes, it's a double-barreled shotgun!"

"What if it is?" Tsvika asked, insulted. "What's wrong with a shotgun? Do you have anything better to suggest?"

"Me? Where would I get anything better? I was just wondering what a shotgun like that was good for."

"What's it good for? For scratching behind my ear! What did you think it was good for, small fry? Guns are for shooting, aren't they?"

"When the skies aren't blue, gray's a fine color, too," said Misha, quoting a proverb.

Avramik frowned. The shortage of weapons had

been worrying him for some time. And now there was confirmation of worse news. "Misha," he said, "is it true that they've taken Naharayim?"

"Yes," said Misha, surprised. "Who told you?"

"Oh, I don't know. There are all kinds of rumors in the trench. And Tsemach, too? We're not holding the police station anymore?"

"No," answered Misha. "But stay calm, Avramik. It'll soon be ours again."

Avramik was not reassured. "That means the Arabs have us surrounded on three sides, doesn't it? Every village in the Jordan Valley . . ."

Misha studied his face. "I can see that you've put two and two together. But don't worry. There are people whose job it is to do that for you. You have my word that the Arabs won't reach our kibbutz."

"Misha, if the high school kids are helping out at the front line, why can't we?" Rina wanted to know.

"You fourth-graders? It looks as though you will have to be evacuated."

"Evacuated?"

"Yes. From the Valley. You'll be moved somewhere safer, perhaps as early as tomorrow."

The two children listened to the news in silence. Roughie was poking about in the bushes again, zigzagging after some invisible creature that was quicker and smarter than he. His brown back appeared and vanished again, gilded by a strong orange light. They all turned to the east to face the rising sun. The mountains of Transjordan stood dark and mute as the huge fireball shot out from behind them into a cloudless sky.

The gray veil of the dawn retreated westward, leaving behind the bright blue of early summer.

"I'm not being evacuated," Avramik declared. "I'm staying here."

He pursed his lips into a thin, determined line whose meaning Misha knew well.

"Do you remember the day I brought you to the kibbutz, Avramik? Those first months?"

Avramik nodded. His eyes were on the ground and his shoulders tensed with a premonition of what would come next.

"You were like a little puppy then, helpless and dependent, like Roughie. You tagged after me day and night. Do you remember?"

Avramik nodded again. Of course he did.

"Good. Well, today you're bigger and stronger, and Roughie depends on you. He's counting on you to make sure he's safe. Do you get me?"

Avramik didn't answer. Misha laid his heavy hands on the boy's shoulders and turned him gently until he was facing him.

"If there's an order to leave, you'll go too, Avramik. And remember, you're responsible for Roughie. He deserves to be out of harm's way as well. Do you promise to look after him?"

Misha raised the boy's chin and looked him in the eyes. He didn't have to wait for an answer. Suddenly, though, he looked up and froze. From the east, out of the sunrise, came a stubborn drone. A terrified Roughie raced out of the bushes and disappeared into the shelter.

156

"Into the shelter!" Misha ordered. "Quickly!"

But the two children remained rooted there, together with Misha and Tsvika. The drone kept coming closer in the fiery sky. Like a mouse transfixed by a snake, like the prey of a hunter, Rina felt unable to move. Now the sound was loud and unmistakable.

"It's a plane!" cried Misha. "A plane!"

The next second he pushed them both into the trench and jumped in after them, pulling Tsvika along.

The plane roared loudly overhead, darkly silhouetted against the blue sky. Something fell out of it, and then something else: black specks that rapidly grew larger until, suddenly, there was a loud boom, followed by another — and then silence. A light brighter than sunlight cast its pitiless glare over everything.

From the bombed barn came a fierce, bitter lowing, a dreadful cry of pain, terror, and protest that reached the far ends of the kibbutz. The flocks of sparrows that had shot into the air with the explosion kept wheeling there, making circle after circle without ever coming down to rest.

30

On May 18, 1948, the Jordan Valley yielded up its children. Three days of bitter fighting had left it no choice. The Syrians had taken the Tsemach police station and were at the gates of Degania, Massada, and Sha'ar Hagolan. The artillery barrages and air raids had put many of the defenders out of action. Large numbers of farm animals were killed or wounded, and the spring flowers in the gardens were buried beneath the rubble of houses. So it was decided to evacuate the villages' most precious possessions, their children.

Every available truck was commandeered for the operation. That, however, did not add up to very many. There was room in them only for the babies, the nursery school children, and the lower grades. Three trucks, covered with canvas tarpaulins, waited at the far end of the kibbutz.

Rika and Alona hurried the fourth grade along. "Let's go, gang! Will everyone please have his clothes bundle ready and be ready himself!"

"I already am!" announced Ofra.

"Me, too!" said Rina. "What should we do now?"

"Whoever's finished can wait on the steps of the shelter."

Several of the children began pushing their way outside.

"And no one leaves without permission," Alona ordered. "It's dangerous. Line up in front of the steps, along the right-hand wall, so that you don't block the passage. And if you hear a siren, get back inside at once, understand?"

"Yes, Alona."

Roughie, who had somehow sensed from the commotion that they were getting ready to leave, bounded up the stairs and vanished through the bright square of the entrance.

"He's run away," cried Rami, starting after him. "Of all the times to decide to run off —"

"Rami, you stay here!" Rika ordered. "Just where do you think he's gone? To Avramik, of course. That's where he always goes."

"That's only because Avramik is outside," said Rami, an old vein of jealousy beginning to throb again. "It's more fun there. That's the reason Roughie goes to him."

"No it isn't," said Giyora, joining the group by the stairs. "It started way before we were ever in the shelter."

For a moment no one said anything. The days before the fighting seemed a long time ago now, more like years than just seventy-two hours.

"Avramik took care of that pup like a mother," said Ofra, breaking the silence. "That's why he's so attached to him."

"I'll bet he would have nursed it if he could," jeered Giyora.

"You shut up," Rami said, his envy turning to guilt. "Don't make fun of him."

"Who's making fun?" Giyora protested. "And who are you to give orders? You'd better remember that you're not the class king anymore!"

"If you wanted to take care of Roughie so badly, Rami, you could have chosen a lower bunk," said Brochi, who rarely opened his mouth. "But you wanted to have a good time, so you left it all up to Rina."

"Hey there, stop quarreling!" called Alona from inside the shelter. "And stop fidgeting, too. I'll be there to count you in a minute."

Mira stopped her in the aisle. "Don't forget Avramik. He's out in the trench with the fifth-graders. They're not being evacuated until tonight, so don't forget him."

"Forget Avramik? How can you even think that?" answered Rika. "You'll see him in a few minutes. We'll all be in the same truck."

It was broad daylight outside. The first summer heat wave had descended on the Valley, and the air was dead, motionless, oppressive, like a furnace being stoked. It seemed to be saying, "Just wait until I show you what I'll do this afternoon. And tomorrow. And the day after that."

The trucks were parked close to the shelter. The toddlers were already inside, safe in their mothers' laps, and now the kindergarten children climbed aboard, making it unbearably hot and crowded. A baby cried.

Rina stared wide-eyed as the open backs of the trucks swallowed more and more children. Amid the chorus of crying infants she heard someone call her name. Stepping closer she saw that it was her little brother Dubik, squeezed among the kindergarten children.

"We're going to Haifa to eat ice cream," he told her, his eyes glowing. "And we'll sleep there in real beds, in a real house."

Rina swallowed hard and said nothing.

"They promised that I could choose any flavor I like," Dubik went on enthusiastically. "My favorite's vanilla. What's yours?"

"It's ..." Rina stammered. "As a matter of fact, it's ..."

Someone stepped up behind her and placed a pair of hands over her eyes. Rina freed herself and turned around to see her mother, surrounded by the kindergarten children like a hen by its chicks. Rina hadn't seen her for ages, not since they had descended to the shelter.

"Ma," she said, searching for words. "Ma ..."

"There's no time, dear," said her mother. "I have to get all these children into the truck. And we're not saying good-bye; we'll be in the same convoy. Hurry up, your class is boarding now. I'll see you soon."

"At the ice cream parlor," shouted Dubik. "We'll see you there, and I'll eat a whole mountain of van —"

From the distance came the sound of an explosion. A machine gun opened fire, and some mortars fired back with a dull thud. Somewhere in the Valley, a kibbutz was fighting for its life.

Rina went to the third truck. The last children were about to climb aboard, among them Avramik. Roughie was cuddled in his arms as if no place could be safer, yet Avramik showed no emotion and kept his eyes on the ground.

The first truck was ready. Its driver raised the tailgate, made it fast, and circled his vehicle for a last, proprietary look. Satisfied with what he saw, he opened the door of the cabin, climbed inside, and switched on the engine.

Then something unexpected happened. From a distant row of young palm trees came a terrible scream, the howl of a wounded animal. Sarah, the kitchen chief, came running toward the truck. The enormous woman charged at it like a mother bear whose cub was being stolen.

"Give me back my little girl," she screamed, hammering on the tailgate. "You murderers! Give her back to me!"

Everyone was too shocked to move. Even the babies stopped crying. Sarah's daughter, a blond little girl, sat on her bundle of clothes with her blue eyes opened wide. Her mother beat on the tailgate with her fists, rattled it, and beat on it some more.

Rina's mother did her best to stay calm. "Sarah," she said, trying to keep her voice level, "Sarah, what are you doing? We're just taking the children to a safe place. We're taking them to where there's no fighting."

Sarah stared at her blankly, as though she had no idea who she was. "They told me that once before, and they took him and never brought him back. Well, it won't happen again. I won't let you! Give me my little girl!"

Rina's mother threw a helpless glance at Misha, who

was equally at a loss as to what to do. "There's an order for just nursing mothers to go in this truck, Sarah," he said. "The other women will leave on foot with the older children tonight. You'll see your girl again tomorrow."

But Sarah was beyond logic.

"All right," said Rina's mother with a nod to Misha. "We'll make room for one more. We'll manage."

Misha lowered the tailgate.

"Up you go, Sarah," he said. "You can be with your little girl. No one's going to take her away from you, never! You're among Jews here. We'll take good care of you both."

Just then there was a yelp of pain. The puppy had fallen from Avramik's arms and, bruised and smarting, lay on the ground. Avramik, who had been watching transfixed, like a man seeing his own past come to life, was shaking all over. He turned and took to his heels as fast as he could.

As though by prior arrangement, Misha and Rina ran after him.

In the tense silence Giyora remarked, "Didn't I tell you he was chicken? I always said —"

But he didn't finish the sentence, for the furious looks aimed at him from all sides made him realize that he had never been more wrong in his life.

31

The trucks traveled slowly along the dirt road. The southern route toward Bet She'an was blocked: the bridge at Naharayim had been blown up, and Naharayim itself had fallen to the Arab Legion, while nearby Gesher was fighting for its life. The northern route toward Tiberias was controlled by the Syrians, who were in command of Tsemach and its police station. There remained only one possibility: the dirt road that ran westward until it joined the paved highway climbing up into the mountains toward Yavne'el.

The trucks jolted along. Rina and Avramik sat side by side near the tailgate of the lead truck. No one ever found out how she and Misha had managed to convince Avramik to board it. Some thought he was a coward and were sure Misha had threatened him with a terrible fate if he remained on the kibbutz. What was to happen later, however, would prove them wrong. Others thought it was because Misha had reminded him of his responsibility for Roughie. The proof, they said, was that as soon as Avramik climbed into the truck he put Roughie in his lap and never let him out of his sight.

The truck was jam-packed. Squeezed into it were

the children of the first four grades, their teachers, and their housemothers. Hardly talking, they sat huddled together on the benches, their bundles in the aisle. The canvas top of the truck hid the view from them and them from all viewers. Not that the convoy was a secret. The Jewish defenders of the Valley had informed the Arabs in advance that the trucks were evacuating children, and both the law of nations and the laws of the human heart forbade their being harmed.

"We're lucky to be sitting in the back," said Rina. "At least we can see out."

Avramik was lost in thought. "What's there to see?" he replied at last, as if it was an effort to bring his mind back to the present. "Look at all the dust we're kicking up."

The hot weather had baked the Valley dry, and the dirt road was already as hard as it would be by the end of the rainless summer. Crawling along like swollen beetles, the trucks churned up a trail of thick dust. Gradually the drivers opened the gaps between them to make the dust less bothersome, and when the lead truck reached the Kinneret-Yavne'el road the others lagged far behind.

"Thank God that's the end of the dust." Rina sighed with relief. "Now we can finally see the Valley. At least we have the Arabs to thank for that," she added, trying to coax a smile out of Avramik. "Look how lovely it is! We haven't hiked here for ages."

Distant and withdrawn, however, Avramik made no reply. No one else talked, either. Worn out from the three days and nights in the crowded shelter, most of the children began dozing off as soon as the truck left the dirt road.

"Some hikers we are. We look more like refugees," thought Rina sadly. "But we'll be back," she suddenly said out loud. "Just see if we won't! Before we know it, it'll all be over and we'll be back in the Valley again."

Avramik petted Roughie with long strokes. "You bet we will!" he said. "And if it takes a while, I'll bring Roughie up and teach him all kinds of tricks. Misha won't recognize him when we get back. He'll be awfully pleased."

From Avramik's thin shoulder, which was pressed against hers, flowed a stubborn determination that Rina knew well.

The truck groaned, shifted gears, and began the ascent to Yavne'el. The last black stone houses of the village of Kinneret dropped away. A dull explosion, followed by a second, sounded in the distance. Far off a machine gun fired a few rounds. Then another. Someone came running from one of the houses in the village, waving his arms at the truck, but they were too far away to make out his shouts. The roar of the motor drowned out everything. One after another, the children fell asleep against each other. Not even Avramik, whose eyes were wide open, had seen the man shouting for them to stop. Half in a trance, he was looking at the view of the Valley below.

Rina pretended to sleep, too. All by itself, it seemed, her head fell heavily onto Avramik's shoulder. A feeling of peace came over her, coursing so sweetly through her body that she could have wished it would go on forever.

Distraught, the man who had run out from the house in Kinneret buried his face in his hands. The second truck had passed him by too, blind to his signals and deaf to his shouts. Only with the third did he succeed. The truck ground to a halt. All its passengers — infants, mothers, children, teachers, housemothers, even a few old grandparents — were quickly unloaded into trenches or made to lie down behind walls and piles of rubble remaining from shelled houses.

The crucial battle for the Tsemach police station had begun, and an inferno of bullets and shells raged for miles around. Nothing was safe from them.

Farther up the mountain, on the road to Yavne'el, the two lead trucks continued to groan wearily beneath their burden, grinding their gears and climbing on, deaf to the sounds of the battle below in the Valley.

Soon, thought their passengers, it would be over. Just a little while longer . . .

32

Avramik had never seen the Sea of Galilee look so peaceful. Like a great big eye, the large lake lay cradled among the mountains, staring up at the blue sky. Large date groves ran down to its shores, while above them cultivated fields made geometric patterns, some the light green of alfalfa, others the yellow of ripe wheat, still others the dark green of vegetables and bananas. Here and there the red roofs of villages could be made out among dense clusters of trees.

To the north, where the river flowed into the smooth, peaceful lake, he could see the vivid green line of the banks of the Jordan. Looking carefully he could detect the river's almost invisible progress through the lake itself until, near Degania, it burst forth from the southern shore in a new line, restlessly following its course amid twisting banks of bulrushes.

As Avramik viewed the panorama below, he felt that something that had been slowly growing within him was finally ripe. Though the feeling had started three years ago, when he first came to the Valley, he had never paid it much attention. Now, however, it was fully grown and had a name: "a sense of belonging," of belonging to the first place he had ever lived in for three whole years; the first place he had ever seen freely, bright in the sunlight, not hunted in the hiding place of a dark cellar; the first place he had ever felt was his home. And with this feeling came a new confidence. "I'll return to the Valley," he told himself. "I'll come home to it again. Wait and see!"

Below, not far from a clump of eucalyptus trees between the river and the lake, thick white puffs of smoke were rising from red-roofed houses, but Avramik, lost in thought, didn't notice. The sound of the truck laboring up the hill drowned out every sound.

Then Avramik saw something flying toward him. Before he could rouse himself it was upon them with a horrible shriek, falling with a tremendous blast not far from the truck. The truck stopped at once, its motor off. The sudden silence was as overwhelming as if the world had burst an eardrum and all sound had ceased to exist. The sleepers awoke; those who had remained awake clutched at their seats. At last, amid the terrifying quiet, Alona's shrill voice was heard to say, "Is anyone hurt?"

Looking around and at themselves, they began to shake off their paralysis. There was blood on Rina's leg. She stared at it incredulously, then tried moving and touching it. Nothing hurt her. She wasn't wounded at all. She turned to look at Rami sitting next to her. A long gash ran down his arm and the blood from it was all over them both. Farther back in the truck Rika was stanching the blood that spurted from a boy's cheek. He wheezed, rasped, and spat out a bloody piece of metal. Shrapnel! Naomi, pale, sat with her hand on one shoulder, thin crimson jets trickling through her fingers and down her arm. Roughie began whimpering and barking, trying to shove his head inside Avramik's shirt.

Alona kept her wits about her. "Everyone off the truck," she ordered. "Into the ditch by the roadside, quickly!"

Her voice was tight but commanding. As though she had been waiting all her life for this moment, she quietly, inarguably, took over.

Clutching Roughie, Avramik was the first over the tailgate.

"Now you," he shouted to Rina. "Don't be afraid. Jump!"

The truck driver ran up, pale and unsteady on his feet, his shirt covered with blood. "Let me open the tailgate," he pleaded weakly. "First let me open it."

Avramik helped him. The gate banged open on its hinges. The driver's knees buckled and he tumbled into the ditch.

"Quick!" shouted Alona in a voice that wasn't hers. "Jump for it, before the next shell lands!"

A horde of children poured onto the road. Some dived into the ditch while others stood there thunderstruck, too terrified to move.

There was a dull whomp as a shell left a distant gun, followed by an approaching whistle.

"Into the ditch!" screamed Alona. "Everyone down!"

The whistle came closer, hideous, ominous, deafening. Rina covered her ears. If only she could crawl into the ground and disappear.

With a great boom the shell exploded across the road, spraying dirt and rocks into the air. They rained down in a quick shower, leaving a crater behind them.

Rina felt fear in every pore of her body. The chill running down her spine made her feel like an icicle. She didn't even notice the rocks and thorns underneath her. But Alona was not going to let them freeze.

"Start running up the hill toward Yavne'el," she yelled. "They're shelling us. Run quickly and keep to the ditch. And when you hear a whistle, hit the ground. Got it?"

"Yes," said Avramik, getting to his feet. His eyes met Alona's. In them was the same quiet determination he had felt earlier in the truck. "Here is one child," thought Alona, "who won't lose his head."

"You lead them up the hill," she said. "I'll stay here with the other grown-ups to care for the wounded."

Rami stood off to the side, staring blankly at the bushes, the drops of blood on his arm sparkling like rubies. Mira rushed up to him. Fumbling in her first-aid kit, she pulled out a gauze bandage.

"Mira, give it to me," said Avramik. "He's all right, it's only a flesh wound. It's dangerous for him to stay here."

Mira hesitated.

"I'll bandage him when we get someplace safe," Avramik promised, and grabbing the pad of gauze, he seized Rami by his good arm and started up the hill with him.

Suddenly it was clear to them all: follow Avramik! He was the only one who knew what he was doing. The children who had been lying in the ditch too frightened to move jumped up and began running after him. Rami stumbled.

"Keep going," Avramik urged. He set Roughie down on the ground and slipped an arm beneath Rami's. For a moment Roughie stood there helplessly, looking about as if making up his mind. Then, leaping forward, he began bounding up the hill, tumbling, falling, and racing upward again on stubby legs, making a beeline for Yavne'el as though he knew just where he was and just where he had to go.

"Follow Roughie," shouted Avramik. "They're zeroed in on the truck. We have to get away from it quickly."

As though to prove him right, a new shell was shrieking horribly toward them. Rina threw herself into the ditch, pressing herself against the ground with her hands over her ears. The shell exploded on the hillside not far away. Clods of earth rained down on their backs.

"Every big kid takes a little one with him," shouted Avramik. "No one gets left behind!"

A small boy lying near Rina began to whimper with fear, curling himself into a ball. "Rina," Avramik called to her, "don't let him lie there. Make him get up and go with you!"

Rina stood up. Avramik's firmness gave her confidence. She knew what she had to do. Her fear was almost gone. Taking the little boy's hand, she made him get to his feet.

"Come on," she said. "Let's run after Roughie. Look how far ahead he is."

The boy gave her a frightened look.

"It's not my fault," he whimpered, his mouth quivering. "It's not my fault . . ."

"Of course it isn't," said Rina. "Roughie just knows the way. He was born in Yavne'el —"

"Not Roughie," said the boy, bursting into tears. "My wee-wee . . . I couldn't hold it in . . . It's not my fault."

"Never mind," Rina said. "It's all right. It'll dry right away. Now give me your hand and let's run after Roughie."

Roughie was far up the hillside, his smooth brown body gleaming on the blacktop of the road.

"Okay," said the boy, starting to walk. "But I'll never catch him. He's running too fast."

"Try anyway," said Rina, pulling him along. "He's leading the way. And when we reach him, he'll let you pet him."

A familiar sound came from the top of the hill. A Jeep was heading toward them from Yavne'el, taking the curves in a hurry. It screeched to a stop by the first group of children.

"Is anyone hurt?" asked the driver.

No one answered. They gaped at the khaki-clad occupants of the Jeep as if they were Martians.

"Are any of you hurt? How about down below by the truck?" asked the driver again.

"Yes," Avramik answered, stepping up to the Jeep without letting go of Rami. "This boy here is hurt, but it isn't serious, just a deep cut. There are some more down below by the truck, but I don't know how many."

"Keep walking!" said the young man beside the

driver. "You're almost out of artillery range. We'll pick up the wounded below and come back to take your friend, too. Just keep on going. There's a truck on its way from Yavne'el to pick you all up."

The Jeep started with a lurch and sped off down the hill. Another shell, lower-pitched and farther off, shrieked. The boom it made came from somewhere between the truck and the last group of children climbing the hill. They were out of danger now.

One by one the children were picked up by the truck from Yavne'el, and in no time the families in the village took them under their wing.

33

Roughie, like a lost son returning home, ran wildly about, stopping to sniff at every gate, yard, and tree in Yavne'el and to lift a leg and pee on them, either from excitement or because he wished to say "Look at me, everyone. I'm back!" Every now and then he scooted off to Avramik, as if to make sure his master hadn't vanished like a passing scent on the breeze, and then he resumed roaming the village.

The children sat on the ground under some thick shade trees. Most of them looked pale and tense. All the food and drink with which the villagers had mothered them had not driven away the shrieks and booms of the shells still echoing in their ears. Some children lay sleeping off their fatigue.

Pigeons were peacefully cooing on the red roof of the infirmary where the wounded were being cared for. His arm in a bandage, Rami stepped out on the front porch. For a moment he stood looking at the children beneath the tree. Then he went and sat down beside Avramik.

"You know, you were right," he said. "I thought you were just trying to calm me, but it really was only a deep scratch, nothing worse."

"What about the others?" asked Rina, who was sitting nearby.

"My mom says that none of them were hurt badly. We really were lucky."

Avramik said nothing. He kept his eyes on the scampering puppy, who never seemed to tire, and away from the children propped on their bundles. They reminded him too much of refugees. Though the danger had passed, he kept reliving the morning of the truck ride. Its memory was like a musical string that wouldn't stop quivering, plucked by an invisible hand.

A horn honked in the distance. Their shell-frayed nerves still on edge, the children awoke and sat up nervously. A Jeep rounded a bend in the road and braked to a halt in front of them. Roughie stood stiffly, then ran to the Jeep with glad yelps, trying frantically to jump in. Two deep barks answered him, and two huge boxers jumped out from the back seat. One, a large, lithe female, began sniffing Roughie and licking him, nuzzling him excitedly with her snout. Shivering with joy he rolled over on his back, baring his tubby belly to the bitch's warm tongue, then jumped up again. The second dog, a powerful, long-legged male, stood watching the commotion as if trying to decide whether to join in the fun or not.

"Well, I'll be. That's Lilith's pup," said the driver of the Jeep. He was a solidly built man of medium height with grizzled hair and a bronzed, deeply lined face, a farmer's face, creased by sun and wind. Bending down to Roughie, he petted him with large, calloused hands that appeared to be permanently stained by machine oil. Lilith kept jumping on the man with her front paws, nearly knocking him over, then turning to lick the ecstatic pup. The man looked at the group of children.

"You must be from Misha's kibbutz, eh?"

"We are," said Rami, getting up. "Don't you recognize me, Yankeleh?"

Bright blue eyes lit up beneath the bushy eyebrows. "Don't I, though! Why, you're Misha's boy Rami!"

"And this is Lilith, Roughie's mother, isn't it? I remember her from when you gave us the puppy. But who's the other dog? Doesn't he belong to Abu-Musa?"

"Right you are. He's Lilith's brother, the uncle of little half-pint over there."

"But what's Abu-Musa's dog doing here?"

"Having a family reunion," said Yankeleh, grinning. "A couple of days before the fighting started down in the Valley, Abu-Musa took his wife and children and went to live in Acre."

"How come?"

"It was too dangerous for him to stay in Adassiya, among all those Jordanians. He has relatives in Acre. He'll be fine there. But he left the dog with me for safekeeping."

Yankeleh looked at Rami attentively. A small blood stain showed through the bandage on his arm.

"Got a scratch there?" he said, half asking, half stating a fact. "I hear you were real lucky."

"It wasn't just luck," declared Rami. "It was also brains and courage. Avramik's. He's the one who got us to Yavne'el."

"We would have been lost without him," Ehud added. "He kept telling us all what to do."

"He's a born leader," Giyora said. "It beats me how he stayed so cool and collected. He'll be a general some day, just see if he won't!"

"Who's Avramik?" asked the man in his deep voice.

Avramik rose, his heart beating fast. That voice reminded him of something, of a distant time and place whose memories were consigned by day to the caverns of oblivion, yet surfaced murkily, tear-swept, in his dreams at night.

"This is Avramik," Rami announced proudly.

Roughie left his mother to caper at Avramik's feet.

"Is the puppy yours?" asked Yankeleh.

"It belongs to all of us," said Avramik in a voice like a stranger's.

Rami bent down to pet Roughie. "But he's Avramik's

most of all," he declared, straightening up again. "He likes Avramik best, and you should have seen him during the shelling."

"Really? What did he do?"

"What did he do? He only led us all to Yavne'el. Roughie showed us the way as though he knew it by heart."

Yankeleh looked at Avramik. He knew that face from somewhere. It reminded him of something. But what?

"I see Lilith's pup has found a good father," he said, slapping the boy on the back. "With his pedigree and the education you're giving him, you're going to have a fantastic dog, a true friend and a loyal watchman, just like his mother and grandmother. All these little mischief makers grow up in the end. How, though, depends on you."

Avramik didn't answer. It wasn't just the voice that was familiar. It was the face, too, which was like the missing part of a puzzle inside him. He needed only one other piece, one other missing clue to complete it.

Yankeleh glanced down at Avramik's Star of David.

"Who gave you that?" he asked in a low voice.

"What's your name?" whispered Avramik.

"Yankeleh. Yankeleh Yisra'eli. Who gave you that Star of David?"

Avramik looked straight into the blue eyes. "You did! Yankeleh Yisra'eli from Yavne'el. The man with the three Y's!"

A shiver ran down Rina's spine. So this was the man Avramik had told her about, whose first and last names and the place he lived all started with Y. This was the man who could tell Avramik the truth about his mother, the only person Avramik would believe, because he had taken her to the hospital and promised to look after her. Promised!

Rina felt her heart in her throat. Now she, too, would know — know the truth about her father and whether to believe those who told her that he had been killed. Here was the man with the three *Y*'s, standing right in front of them.

Avramik licked his lips, which were as dry as parched earth.

"My mother," he whispered. "What happened to her?"

Yankeleh placed two large, loving hands on the boy's shoulders. "She . . ." He paused. "She died in the hospital."

"Died?" said Avramik, almost inaudibly. "My mother's dead?"

"Yes," said Yankeleh, his voice choked with emotion. "I never had a chance to tell you because my unit was transferred soon afterward. Later I tried looking for you, but you were no longer in the refugee camp."

Avramik's dark eyes opened wide, like portholes peering into some deep mystery. His face twitched. He spun around and ran toward the infirmary just as the front door opened and Mira, his aunt, stepped outside. For a moment she just stood there, too stunned to react. Then she opened her arms to catch the sobbing child.

No one saw exactly what happened next, because everyone was crying: children, mothers, grandparents, all had tears in their eyes. Rina wept on Yankeleh's shoulder. This time she had to believe. She knew she would never see her father again, never. Other children cried to release the accumulated tension and fear, the horror of the shrieking shells. Sarah, the kitchen chief, hugged her little daughter and began to weep too, as did all the toddlers and babies. And then the skein of horror snapped and was gone. The wave of crying subsided, yielding to the solace of a great serenity. The bitter tears became sweet and warm, because Roughie was running excitedly about and trying to lick all their faces. They could feel the heavy lumps in their throats being carried off and swept far away.

"Go ahead, cry," said Yankeleh, stroking Rina's hair. "It's all right; it's nothing to be ashamed of. Even heroes sometimes cry."

Avramik clung to Mira for a long while. Then, wiping his face with the back of his hand, he turned to face the others. Looking back at him, they saw something they had never seen before: the inner peace of a person who has been put to the test and has not been found wanting.

"Never mind," he said. "We'll be back in the Valley, you'll see. We'll be back before long and we'll never leave it again. Never!"

Roughie looked up and barked his agreement. No one doubted for a moment that Avramik's words would come true.

Epilogue

By the end of that summer the children were back in the Jordan Valley, and, indeed, they left it no more. Many years went by and big oaks grew from little acorns.

Roughie, the merry, loyal little pup, became a big, strong boxer, the finest dog on the kibbutz, but he still followed Avramik around like a shadow. Roughie's grandchildren play with Rina and Avramik's children, and anyone who asks where they are is told with a smile, "Ah, the boxer family. Who doesn't know where to find them? Just go to the main lawn, and when you see a big heap of children and dogs all romping together, you're there!"